Towards the end of another day, Will stepped outside to survey the men's work. They'd completed the palisade in front of the house and along its two sides, and only the back remained to finish. Will stalked the perimeter with his flintlock in his belt, considering the craftsmanship and strength of the structure. Already, the thing had given him confidence. Already, he felt...

An agonizing pain lanced through his left shoulder from behind, followed by a line of fire across his ribs on the opposite side. An instant later, he heard a loud thud and spied an arrow, newly stuck into the side of the cottage. Will spun, taking an arrow in the left forearm and fired his pistol into the tall grass near the forest. Before he hit the ground himself, he heard a loud scream of pain, which brought a brief smile to his lips. Rushing to reload his pistol, his own labored breathing roared in his ears, and his heartbeat throbbed behind his eyes. More arrows were coming, he was certain. Arrows and then spears and, finally, clubs.

Margaret's voice called out to him from the front side of the cottage. While he was relieved that she was aware something was amiss, he did not want her to sustain any further injuries, and so he kept quiet, peering eastward into the trees. *Is this how it ends?* He thought he heard the grunts and subdued groaning of someone grievously hurt, but trying to keep his position a secret. There were words exchanged, also, but too low and faint to be understood.

"Will!" Margaret gasped. Though she approached from behind, he could well guess the expression on her face. "Bastards!" she exclaimed. And, "Don't move; I'll help you." Again, he wanted to warn her away, but he knew it was futile.

THIS THING
OF
DARKNESS

ALLAN BATCHELDER

For my dad.

Sonnet 66

Tired with all these, for restful death I cry,
As to behold desert a beggar born,
And needy nothing trimm'd in jollity,
And purest faith unhappily forsworn,
And gilded honour shamefully misplac'd,
And maiden virtue rudely strumpeted,
And right perfection wrongfully disgrac'd,
And strength by limping sway disabled
And art made tongue-tied by authority,
And folly—doctor-like—controlling skill,
And simple truth miscall'd simplicity,
And captive good attending captain ill:
Tir'd with all these, from these would I be gone,
Save that, to die, I leave my love alone.

~ 1 ~

THE WILD AND WASTEFUL OCEAN

Somewhere in the Atlantic, April, 1619

The dead man cowered in his bunk as the ship about him lurched and groaned on the storm-churned sea. The hull growled, the timbers whined, and the masts protested endlessly. Between blasts of thunder and the crashing of waves upon the deck above, the man could hear the shouts and cries of the crew and his fellow passengers. *Wouldn't it be ironic if we all went down?* He thought. *And for me, of all people. Full fathom five, indeed.* Not that anyone would mourn his loss, since most who cared about him had already shared their grief back in England. Still, it would be sad to sink to the bottom of the Atlantic unnoticed, except by his bastard son, struggling to sleep in own bunk, and the other men on board, who couldn't tell him from their favorite tapster for all the gold in America.

Abruptly, the ship rolled to starboard, throwing the frightened passenger onto the rough-planked floor of his cabin, where he lay, panting, like a terrified house cat, until the vessel corrected itself and he tumbled back in the other direction. He locked eyes with his now-awake son for an instant and saw his own terror reflected back at him, despite the darkness of the room.

"All's well!" the man exclaimed, as he dragged himself back into his bunk. "Happens all the time!" If only he could sleep— not the eternal sleep threatened by this angry ocean, but simple sleep, sleep that knits up the raveled sleeve of care and so forth. He'd have paid any amount to doze through this tempest and awaken on the other side, in calmer seas, with a bit of blue sky overhead. He knew he owed God a death; he just hoped it wasn't due yet.

Still, as much as he feared for his life and that of his boy, he was even more concerned for the safety of his books. His body, after all, was merely a vessel—much like this ship—but his books! His books were the children of his spirit, and...there the metaphor fell apart, like bread in wine. He would like to have gone into the hold, to ensure that his cargo was secure and dry, but candles and lamps were undoubtedly out all over the boat and, with its violent jostling, the man didn't think such a journey likely to end in success.

As if on cue, the ship listed dangerously to port. A dog, belonging to one of the other passengers, yelped in terror, and the frightened passenger ruminated on how fear was a great equalizer amongst animals, making a man no better than a rat, or, alternatively, making them comrades-in-arms, in their battle against a common, implacable foe. If only they could take arms against *this* sea of troubles and by opposing, end them. Or it.

There came a blast of thunder so loud that he nearly soiled himself. It would be a wonder if the masts hadn't been shattered to kindling. He'd had many a long night over his fifty-some years, but he promised the gods above and below he would never take His or Their names in vain again, if only they'd see him safely to shore this one last time.

Fretting and sweating in his bunk, he finally fell asleep.

He was awakened sometime later by a sharp noise at his door. With a glance, he confirmed the sound had likewise roused his son, and that someone had forced his way into their presence amidst a veritable cloud of Rhenish vapors.

"Do as I say, and no one gets hurt!" the shadow commanded.

The dead man frowned in disappointment. "That's the best you can do?"

"Shut up and toss your purse my way, along with anything else o' value."

"You are drunk, sir. How do you expect to escape justice on this wee boat with nowhere to hide?" the dead man demanded incredulously.

"That's my concern. Now, I won't ask again. Your valuables. Now."

Once more, the dead man glanced over at his son, who huddled quietly in his bunk. With a long-suffering sigh that projected a confidence he did not feel, he pulled his pistol from beneath his blanket and fired at the intruder, who flew backwards into the wall and immediately collapsed. Frightened by the blast, the boy leapt to his feet.

"Don't trouble yourself, lad. I'm just ridding the ship of its rats. One of them, anyway."

Anon, there came a stern knocking on the door. "That's the Captain and his men, I expect," he said to his son, who had returned to his previous position. In the next motion, he crossed to the door and pulled it open. In the corridor, the First Officer and several of the crew stood with weapons ready.

"We heard gunfire," the First Officer deadpanned.

~ 2 ~

SO QUICK, BRIGHT THINGS
COME TO CONFUSION

Virginia's Jamestown Colony, April, 1619

There is something enormously gratifying about splitting firewood, about using an axe with such violence and precision, about exercising one's muscles in the out-of-doors, providing one's family with the fuel necessary to cook its food and keep it warm. All in all, it was one of Jamieson's favorite tasks, and this evening was no different. To his left, his eldest picked up and stacked the newly split logs under the eaves of the family home, that they might age and dry until needed. Well off to Jamieson's right, his two daughters frolicked amongst the wildflowers, far enough away to stay clear of the axe or any of the splinters its work might send flying, but near enough that Jamieson might reach them should the need arise.

He paused in his labors to wipe the sweat from his brow with the back of his left arm.

"Are we done, papa?" his son asked hopefully.

Jamieson smiled. Terrence reminded him of himself as a boy, always looking for a chore to be done as quickly as possible. "I'll cut a few more, yet," he responded. He still had some minutes before sunset, and he wanted to accomplish as much as possible before that nonnegotiable deadline.

Terrence sighed just loudly enough for his father to hear, but said nothing. He, too, was aware that sundown would bring an end to this task and the welcome advent of dinnertime, card games, and stories. Some of those stories, no doubt, would be about what happened to those who dared to stay out after dark, for it was well known that although the Powhatans were not the most aggressive of the local natives (nor yet the most agreeable), there were others who might think nothing of capturing or killing a settler's child. These stories terrified his sisters, but Terrence loved them. He wasn't afraid of the natives, at least not while he was indoors, and his father's musket stood ready for firing.

Long, long seconds later, Terrence heard his father lay the axe against the stump he used for splitting. He turned to see him take in the lowering sun.

"It's about that time," he said regretfully. Lord, how the man loved to work! "Girls!" he called. "Let us go inside. Terrence, be a good lad and bring the axe, will you?" Without waiting for a response, Jamieson looked over at the cottage and began to walk towards it.

His daughters, Meredith and Alice, were quick to obey their father's commands, but Terrence was a bit slower in complying. He wasn't allowed to use the axe just yet, but with his father's back turned, he could not resist an errant swing or two. Just let one of the natives try him now! He'd chop 'em to kindling.

"Terrence!" his father barked from the cottage door.

Of course. The man heard and saw everything. It was a blessing, his mother said, for the family but certainly a curse for young Terrence. He lowered his eyes sheepishly, slumped his shoulders, and carried the axe as he'd been taught. A lecture was coming, he knew, and a stern one at that.

Inside, the children's mother was laboring over the stew pot when she suddenly cried out in pain. Jamieson, who'd just begun the process of barring the door, rushed to her side to determine the cause of her distress. The ladle, it seemed, had been too close to the flames, so that when she picked it up, she seared her fingers and the palm of her hand but good. Her husband poured cool water upon the burn and carefully wrapped the hand in linen.

"Wash up, now," Terrence's mother told him and his sisters, who stood by gawking. "It's just a burn. Happens all the time."

Salted pork. How Terrence hated it. He would have given anything for a bit of venison. Alas, salted pork was what there was, and it was that or nothing, as his father so often reminded him. Still, Terrence would rather have eaten his shoe. He glanced across the table and saw his father glaring at him—did the man ever do anything else? Hoping to appease him, Terrence shoved a goodly bite of meat into his mouth and chewed, careful to keep any sign of disgust from his face.

"I was thinking," said Jamieson to no one in particular, "of building a smokehouse, 'twould give our meat a bit more flavor and make the fish and fowl last longer. I'll be needing some help, of course..." He let the last trail off, but his son knew exactly who the help was meant to be and couldn't have been happier.

"I can do it!" he volunteered, a little too lustily.

His sisters giggled and his mother fought back a chuckle herself, even as she winced at the lingering pain in her hand. "Just you finish your supper first!" she scolded gently.

That task accomplished and everything tidied up, the family gathered near the hearth, to enjoy a few songs and fables by the fire. Only, Jamieson could not locate his pipe for his customary postprandial smoke. He checked and rechecked his pockets. He searched the table. He scanned the hearth.

"Ye left it outside, papa!" Terrence reminded him. "By the chopping block."

"Did I?" Jamieson asked in obvious disappointment. "Well, I suppose I'll have to do without—"

But his son, eager for his father's approval, rushed to the door Jamieson had never quite finished locking, threw aside the bar, and rushed out into the darkness.

In a panic, Jamieson and his wife dashed after their son, calling his name and demanding he return. They were stopped cold by a terrible roar unlike any sound they'd ever heard. "It's a bear!" Jamieson cried out, but he didn't believe it. As he turned to fetch his musket, he was hit in the back by something heavy and hard that knocked him onto his belly. His wife and daughters screamed and continued to scream. Jamieson rolled over and saw Terrence's bloody head on the floor to his left, gazing over at him with a look of utter confusion and be-damned if the lips weren't moving! "Shut the door!" Jamieson yelled to his wife, the only one close enough to manage it.

But it was already too late.

~ 3 ~

RIPENESS IS ALL

The Atlantic Ocean, April, 1619

The fact that he woke up the next morning struck him as nothing less than miraculous. In the first place, he was astounded to discover he'd actually fallen asleep again; in the second, the ship was still afloat. His left knee ached, but that was nothing new. And his belly burned something terrible. That little concern would kill him in earnest someday, he'd no doubt, but evidently today was not that day.

He glanced about his cabin. It was little more than a closet, but that 'little more' was much more than the rest of the passengers enjoyed. Such, the prerogatives of wealth. He pondered that wealth, his son, and the time ahead. He knew the days of his second life were dwindling rapidly, and that his next death would be final. And so, he wanted to live, truly live, in the time remaining to him. After his funeral (which he'd attended in disguise), he traveled, just as he had in his youth, in his salad days. But although unknown to him, everywhere he went was nevertheless known by and to *someone*, and he left each location a little dismayed at the lack of surprise. America, on the other hand, was full of still-unexplored forests, mountains, meadows and lakes. The dead man wanted to see the 'ugly' mermaids of which he'd heard tell. He wanted to see the savages who skulked about the primordial woodlands. He wanted to see trees that had never known the axe and rivers that had never been fished. And to greet this New World, he had become a new man.

Nowadays, he called himself William Kemp. He was

comfortable enough with William, and being William Kemp made him laugh, as the real William Kemp never had. Not that anyone on board or in the New World would know the difference, and, in fact, the new William Kemp was counting on it. He was somewhat disappointed to discover no women dressed as men amongst the other passengers (a favorite fantasy of his), but he *did* encounter a man dressed as a woman who called herself Margaret. Will had seen many such men in his time, and Margaret's effort was especially refined, despite her rather hulking size. He thought, whimsically, that he might marry her, if only to cement their two disguises with further authenticity. Nothing convinced like the veneer of domesticity.

Such musings naturally put him in mind of his actual wife, the poor, forlorn victim-of-all victims he'd gradually learned to despise, largely because of how she made him feel about himself. He had been—was!—a man of great accomplishment, but in her eyes, he was a faithless husband, a poor father, and a terrible drunk, which insult hurt worse than the other two combined. In his mind, he was an excellent drunk. *Quam bene vivas referre, non quam diu.*

She was a right Christian martyr, though—at least she thought herself to be, never mind that he'd brought much wealth and luxury into her life, wealth and luxury she could never have expected at the time of their marriage. As a provider, he'd exceeded expectations to the same degree that the sun exceeds a candle. But she always wanted more of him—more intimacy, more time, more conversation and, most especially, more frequent attendance at church. He was like his father in that regard, however, and would rather have listened to the slaughter of swine for all eternity than spend another moment in the pews. Besides, he'd spent the better part of his life listening to the greatest orators in the land; the pastor at his local church was a poor substitute.

He'd been glad to say goodbye to his town, as well. In retirement, he'd been beleaguered by folks angling for loans, for gifts, for his benison. None of them really seemed to know him or his work, none seemed to have any genuine feelings for him outside of jealousy. As a boy and young man, he'd always thought his town too small, too provincial. He was more than sorry that his retirement had confirmed it. And so, he was saddled with a wife, a home, and a town that no longer brought him the least bit of satisfaction, of joy. What was to be done? Now a man of title and reputation, he could not simply leave. The scandal would have been too great for someone whose continued income depended upon public adoration. Fortunately, his own works instructed him, and he contrived to fake his own death.

"Good morrow, Master Kemp," the first mate said as Will emerged onto the deck.

"As I am still alive to see it, yes, 'tis very good, indeed. And please, there's no need to call me Master Kemp. Will is more than adequate."

"As you say, Will. The captain would like a word."

He was no seer, Will, but he'd been expecting as much and imagined he could probably predict the ensuing conversation to the last detail.

"Master Kemp," the captain would say. "You shot and killed a man aboard my ship last night."

"Only after he broke into my quarters and threatened my apprentice and me."

"That's as may be," the captain would offer, "but I cannot have my passengers murdering one another, even in self-defense. Why didn't you shoot him in the shoulder, or the leg? How am I to question his corpse?"

The actual conversation was little different, save for one small but vital detail: the dead man was one of parolees from Newgate Prison, and was sure to have had friends both onboard and in Jamestown.

Will, it seemed, had kicked the proverbial hornets' nest.

~ 4 ~

I SHALL NO MORE TO SEA, TO SEA—
HERE SHALL I DIE ASHORE!

Jamestown Colony, April, 1619

The fog fell away almost coyly, like a new bride disrobing for her husband on their wedding night and revealed a dark shape against the horizon. The New World! Nothing had captured his imagination so since he was a boy watching pageant plays in his village and dreaming of bigger things in London. Even as his eyes beheld it, he had difficulty believing it. How was it possible that such a land had existed unknown for so long? The mystery of it all thrilled and frightened him. Soon, very soon, he would disembark and take his first steps in a place few Europeans had ever visited. It was likely, in his wandering, his feet would find virgin soil, where no one of any sort had ever walked—not Alexander, not Caesar, not even His Majesty. Oh, Raleigh had made a cursory sort of exploration, but surely there were untold acres, whole countries of land that he'd never seen.

Will was no fool, however, and he knew there would be dangers, both unfathomable and mundane. That was why he'd purchased his flintlock pistol—the very latest thing—along with a musket, and brought along a brace of daggers and his rapier. He was not a young man, could not pass for one in anyone's company, but he would not be taken or taken advantage of easily. Whoever dared try was in for a terrible surprise. Or so he hoped.

Gradually, he became aware of his fellow passengers

gathering on either side of him, each of them seemingly as lost in his own thoughts as Will himself had been seconds earlier. If anyone could gaze upon America and not feel shaken, inspired, and astounded, that person was dead inside.

"I wonder if them savages is watchin' us," the man to his left said.

"Ah," Will answered, "but we'll be watching them back, won't we?"

The other man scoffed. "Yes, but they know where we are! We can't see them, yet!"

"Thank God for your yelling, then."

The other man's jaw snapped shut with an audible click and then, after a moment, he muttered, "Damned gentlemen…" before wandering off.

On Will's right, another man chuckled and said, "I'll be amazed if that one lasts a week."

Will smiled and nodded back at the fellow, but had no interest in further conversation. He'd endured a lifetime of talk and was looking forward to a little silence once he got ashore. Instead, it seemed the perfect time to enjoy his pipe. He was nearly out of tobacco, but that was one thing, he understood, that the New World had in abundance. Perhaps he would even grow some himself—he didn't need the money, but a man wanted a hobby, didn't he? And, at his age, hunting was probably out of the question.

A vast gap on the approaching coast gave evidence of a river mouth—the James River, in fact—and a well-named river it was, too, since, like its namesake at a public speaking event, it seemed to go on and on. Will chuckled. He wondered if, even here, he was far enough from England to say such things aloud. Probably not, he guessed.

As the ship progressed upriver, Will noted the James was much greener in hue than the Thames—a brownish-gray on the best of days and ofttimes full of refuse. There was none in the James, however, and Will could actually see great fish leaping from its waters upon occasion. Into this reverie stepped his son, again. Will had been putting off certain necessary discussions with the young man, but they could not be avoided forever.

Best, he thought, to have it all over with, so that dread of its coming did not dampen his enjoyment of whatever the New World had to offer.

"Son," he said, in acknowledgment of the boy's presence.

"I have a name," the boy answered gruffly.

"That you have. The name of my dearest friend as it happens, and also of my brother. I'd have chosen something else for you, had I been consulted."

"What?"

"I might've called you Edward, I think, or Alexander."

The boy hunched over the rail, was quiet a moment, and then said, "Not even William?"

"Gods, no! You're no mere copy of your father, whatever else you may be."

"Alexander was a king, wasn't he?"

"An emperor!" Will beamed.

Nodding to himself, the boy said, "Then call me Xander, if Richard likes you not."

"Xander it is. A new name, for a New World!" It was no less than he'd done himself, anyhow. For all that, his son was dark-skinned—black, like his mother—and Will was uncertain how the boy might be received by the people of Jamestown. And then, as the father of such a child, well, he was not exactly above judgment, either, was he? "It is just possible," he said to his son, "that the people of this New World will not look favorably upon us as individuals or a pair. We may alleviate some scrutiny if we pretend that you are my servant or apprentice instead of my son."

Xander frowned at this, but said nothing as he considered the matter. At length, he declared, "I'll play that part, but don't you forget what you've promised me."

"Never," Will agreed.

This James River was so wide in places that its far shore was nothing more than a line of shadow across the horizon, and it was not difficult to imagine that such a vast and powerful tributary might indeed run all the way to China. But that was beyond Will's interest. Having been aboard the George for six weeks, he desired nothing more than landfall and a bed that did not list to-and-fro with every breeze. Jamestown, the captain had told him, was still two or three days upriver, though. He would therefore have to content himself with richly-scented air, redolent of fir, oak and alder, of grasses and sweet, ripe earth. And, of course, the river itself. Even the Avon had never smelled so good.

Looking about himself, it was evident that his fellow passengers were of his mind, for the deck was nearly packed to capacity with those fleeing the horrid confines below decks.

It had become something of a ritual for the mysterious Margaret to acknowledge his presence whenever she was nearby. Sometimes, this was done through the slightest of nods; on other occasions, she walked to his side and inquired as to his health and frame of mind. There was, Will noted, a connection there, an understanding of some sort, and more and more he believed they were destined to become friends, though the particulars remained unclear to him. In light of this possibility, he felt it past time to introduce his son.

"Isn't the air just lovely?" he asked Margaret by way of greeting. Before she could answer, he said, "There's someone I'd like you to meet. Richard!" he called over his shoulder to the boy, who leaned upon the rail some ten paces distant.

"Xander," his son reminded him.

"Yes, yes," Will replied, "Margaret, this is my apprentice, Xander."

"Pleased to meet you," Margaret said, nodding in Xander's direction.

"You look like one of my mum's companions," the boy declared, sharing just the tiniest taste of his Southwark dialect.

Will blushed in embarrassment at the boy's forwardness, but Margaret merely raised an eyebrow in his direction. "Is that a good thing, or a bad?" she asked him.

"Oh! Pardon!" said Xander. "A good, a good. They're as kind and true a bunch as you could hope to meet."

Margaret and Will both smiled at the boy's recovery. "Then I hope I *shall* meet them, one day," Margaret replied.

Will didn't think it likely but kept that to himself.

The big day arrived.

Gazing at the shore again, Will could at last see evidence of a settlement 'round the next bend, the very town where this ship was meant to dock. Small towns and villages in England had buildings of stone, despite their diminutive size. This village, from all he could see, had no such buildings, and even the streets were dirt. There would be no luxuries, then, no convenience. At least not for the foreseeable future. But it was nothing more or less than Will had expected, which was why a goodly portion of the ship's cargo belonged to him. He'd even brought along his customary bed, which he'd had stolen from his wife at the time of his death, under the pretext of leaving it to his surviving child and her husband. It would never arrive at her home. Call him a bastard, but if he was going to begin a new life in a relative wilderness, he was damned-well going to have a good night's sleep.

The ship's bell rang out behind him, startling him from his daydreaming. An answering bell chimed from the shore and all about him, Will saw the crew rushing to their various stations. The rest of the passengers appeared as well, some with sleep still in their eyes, others, already carrying everything they'd brought along and anxious to disembark. Will was in no rush. His belongings would take a while to offload, and, anyway, he never liked being part of the frantic throng.

What though it all seemed a fantasy, a strange fever dream, Jamestown itself looked very real indeed. And now that he saw it, Will wondered again at the rumors of cannibalism, of Spanish spies, of hostile natives, and more. At one point, the people of Jamestown had even been ravaged by the plague. It was an ancient enemy, the plague, but no less deadly for all that. He'd lost loved ones, family and friends to it, and yet he endured. Why? It was a question he'd asked himself countless times over the years; he'd given up hope of ever finding an answer.

While the majority of those on board continued to crowd the rail, Will crossed the deck and gazed out into the woods along the shore, hoping to see the birds or animals of the New World. The crush of humanity no longer held interest for him.

He might well and truly have declared, "Man delights not me." But to glimpse creatures he'd never before seen? He had no greater desire.

"And where will you go from here?" a familiar voice asked. Will turned slightly to see Margaret standing not three paces away, leaning against her own section of rail.

"I've rented an empty cottage for a fortnight or two. I'd like to get the lay of the land before making any further plans. You?"

The man who was Margaret smiled. "I don't rightly know. I'm looking for lodgings myself, and, from there, who can say?"

"If I decide to build in town, you're welcome to claim one of my rooms," Will said, thinking of his earlier notion. "Might be safer for you."

"Ah," Margaret grinned, "but will be it be so for you?" She arched an eyebrow at him, and he found himself blushing, in spite of his experience.

"I am not worried," he answered.

They chatted in this manner for some time, until the captain approached and informed them that all their belongings had been carried ashore and were ready to be claimed.

"Alexander!" Will called to his son, "go and see if there's anyone in town willing to haul our belongings thither for a fee." To Margaret, he said, "I should have thought there'd have been someone here for the purpose, but it appears Jamestown is even more rustic than advertised." He shrugged. "But it's all one, isn't it? We came looking for the brave New World, the unpredictable and unexpected, and so it presents itself in the tiniest of details."

In time, Xander returned, empty-handed and alone, looking much perturbed.

"Yes?" Will asked him.

"Most of the people I met wouldn't trade two words with me."

Will had an inkling as to why this might be so and expected the boy did as well, but refrained from sharing his thoughts. There would be time for such a discussion after they'd settled in. He was roused from further musings by the approach of a horse-drawn wagon, driven by an old man and a boy of no more than ten. Taken aback by this rather underwhelming welcome, Will asked, "Where is everyone?"

The old man chuckled through a nearly toothless grin. "Come and gone," said he. "As you must have seen. Folks get so excited when new supplies arrive, they can't hardly wait to unpack 'em."

It seemed Will had lingered too long. "Can you help my apprentice and me then?"

"'S what I'm here for."

With that, the old man and his son climbed down and started to grapple with the various crates, finally seizing on the largest.

"What's this, then? A bed?"

"It is," said Will. "It will undoubtedly require all of us to get it onto your wagon."

The old man shook his head. "Gentlemen," he muttered dismissively. It seemed a common complaint.

Both locals and all three arrivals did indeed have to lend their muscles to the task of loading the bed. But that was not the end of their durance. A large, square box proved equally unwieldy for the old man and son. As they struggled and stumbled with their burden, Will called out, "Careful with that crate, there. It's valuable."

"Gods, it's heavy," the old man replied. "What's in it, cobblestones?"

"Books."

The man scoffed. "Books? Valuable? For what, kindling?"

Margaret elbowed the man aside and hefted the entire load onto the cart by herself, eliciting gasps of surprise from both locals. Even Will was impressed.

"I packed that crate," said he. "It's got to be twice the weight of a man!"

Margaret shrugged. "A woman in my...situation...can't afford to be weak." Not wishing to say more, she attacked the rest of the baggage with near maniacal attention until the task was complete.

"Where to?" the old man asked, after climbing back into his seat at the front of the wagon.

"I've rented Turnby's cabin, for the short term."

"Turnby's, is it?" the boy said. "Good luck."

Will frowned. If these two were indicative of the rest of Jamestown's inhabitants, it was just possible he'd made a mistake in coming hither.

The old man spat from his perch. "Wanna hop on up here?"

None of the new arrivals did.

"Suit yourselves."

Despite his bad feet and dodgy knee, it was no kind of walk from the ship, through the heart of Jamestown, and into its outskirts—such as they were, and Will was glad he'd disembarked last, for the other passengers had flooded the main street of the village and provided enough distraction that Will and his companions were able to pass by without trouble or interruption.

"How many people call Jamestown home?" Will asked of the old man.

"There's nigh onto seven, eight hundred hereabouts. Almost a thousand throughout Virginia. Settlers, I mean. Of savages, there's many thousand more."

Will very much doubted he'd see any of the native folk in the near future. It was said they kept mostly to themselves and only appeared if the English encroached on their territory or they found reason to trade.

He pondered the elasticity of words upon first sighting the alleged cottage. Yes, it had four walls, a roof and a door. But so did a shed, a barn, a mausoleum. He supposed the word cottage could be stretched to fit the thing before him, but whoever had done so initially was either possessed of a most bountiful imagination or else no morals whatsoever. Without saying a word, he walked about the structure. It looked more suited to storing onions than housing anyone, but, as he'd oft noted, there was small choice in rotten apples.

Onions. Apples. Was he hungry?

His son looked over at him imploringly, clearly hoping that Will would opt to lodge elsewhere.

"T'will serve, for the nonce," said he. "Until we can find or build something better." Acknowledging the pained look in his son's eyes, he said, "You've slept in worse places, surely?"

"Yes," the lad admitted, "but not by choice." After a pause, he added, "Why is it so much worse than the others? D'you suppose someone died in it?"

"Is there a better place to die than in one's own home? I've seen men die on the battlefield, in the streets, even in taverns. None of them looked at peace to me."

Xander sighed. This was not an argument he could win.

"You'll stay with us?" Will turned to Margaret.

"I'd be delighted," she answered, without the slightest trace of irony or sarcasm. "We can make this thing livable," she said to Xander. "Just you wait and see!"

In the end, the job took a couple of weeks' hard labor, 'round the clock, but even Xander had to admit it was worth it. The Turnby place would never serve as a permanent residence, no—it was too small and too close to town for that—but it was more than adequate for a short-term stay. The windows were situated such that the cottage received maximum sunlight, so that it didn't seem anywhere near as dark and smoky as most such lodgings. The neighbors, for the most part, were friendly but kept to themselves, busy with planting, or tending their crops, dressing their game or other suchlike activities. Some there were, of course, who regarded Will and his companions with suspicion, and he was not surprised. A wealthy old gentleman, a black boy, and a man who dressed and behaved like a woman were a most unusual trio in anyone's experience. Will didn't care overmuch what his new countrymen thought, but he suspected that some would get used to him and his friends, while others would simply nurse their preconceptions.

Will never stopped searching for better lodgings, however, as per his promise to young Xander. There was no shortage of land to be had, either—if a man had no fear of the natives—but though he cherished his privacy, Will was unwilling to separate himself completely from potential allies. Thus, he made inquiries whenever he walked into town to purchase or barter for supplies. The locals, naturally, were quite curious about him and his companions, the woman being, after all, quite large for her gender, and the boy being so dark-skinned.

But it was clear, too, that Will was a man of means, even if he eschewed the attire most typical of his station. Apparel oft proclaims the man, yes, but so do bearing, behavior and speech. And Will possessed the skills—or talents, really—to seem other than he was, to seem more salt-of-the-earth, and thus many of the locals both sought his business and trusted his intentions.

Eventually, he came upon a group of men discussing a massacre and could not help listening in. He'd assumed it was to do with the natives, but no, this was something else altogether.

"Still haven't found her head," a tall, gaunt fellow said.

"And the son's?" asked a shorter, stouter man with a bulbous nose.

"Under the table, as I heard it."

"Worst part," a woman interjected, "was Jamieson's entrails drug all over the place."

"That don't sound like no Powhatans to me."

"Nor me."

"Shame," said the woman. "It's such a lovely home."

Will could not resist. "Trouble with the natives?"

"No, no," the tall man replied. "A bear maybe, or a pack o' wolves."

"Bears don't decapitate folk," the shorter man countered.

"How did these animals get inside?" Will asked.

"Nobody knows," said the woman. "Shame, too. Such a lovely family. A lovely home."

Without trying to come off as too eager or insensitive, Will asked, "And, eh, just where is this home?"

The tall man blinked. "Oh, right, you've just arrived. You wouldn't know, would you?" He took a deep breath as if he were about to recite epic poetry and launched into an explanation of how the home could be found. It was a ways out of town, but a horse could reach it in five minutes at a gallop. Far away enough for privacy, close enough that gunshots could still be heard in Jamestown. Here, he suspected, was a real estate bargain waiting to be snapped up by the first man with money.

Of course, he needed to see it first.

~ 5 ~

WE HAVE SEEN BETTER DAYS

Southwark, March, 1619

He'd heard she was dying, and he could not stay away. The other girls led him to her chamber, where he discovered her in bed, reeking of death, terribly gaunt, gazing out the window to her left. Gradually, she became aware of his presence and turned her head ever-so-slowly, gingerly, in his direction. Seeing him, she said nothing for what seemed the longest time, and then, wryly, "Will you look what the cat dragged in!"

He wanted to laugh, oh, how he wanted to. But seeing her in such a state robbed him of his voice.

"You've put on weight," she said.

And you've lost too, too much.

"Where be your gibes now? Your gambols? Your songs? Your flashes of merriment that were wont to set the table on a roar?" she taunted.

Now he smiled. "I've always envied your memory."

"You would not do so now."

There was some sort of accusation there, he knew, and he certainly deserved it, whatever the particulars.

"So," she said, "what's it like, being dead?"

She was angry, bitter, frightened. *Where to begin?* He wondered. *And how to end?* They could never have an honest conversation as long as he remained on the defensive. "As I recall," he said, "it was *you* told *me* to fuck off. Which I did."

She closed her eyes and grinned, but it was a tight, painful thing. "And you took it so absolutely." After an interminable pause, she went on, "I sought elevation. Can you blame me? What other recourse has a woman—an *African* woman—in London? You might have been the man."

"My wife..."

"Ha! Your *wife*! And where is she now? Dead, too?"

Will shook his head. "She lives. As far as I know."

She chuffed in judgment. "Men."

He crossed to the bed and took her hand, naught now but a collection of brittle twigs in a leathern pouch. Still, she squeezed his hand in return. "I've missed you."

"And I, you. Every minute of every day. And the nights? Unspeakable."

She paused. "I am afraid."

He sat next to her, as carefully, as gently as he could. "Yes."

"You must do me one favor."

"Of course."

"You must take my son with you—as your apprentice, your squire, your...what you will."

He smiled, again, at her little jest. He'd not known she had a son, but it made sense. He was flattered, insulted, terrified all at one go. "I don't think that..."

"You must!" Luce insisted. "For the love you once bore me. If you do not, this place will be the end of him."

It was too much to ask; too much to deny. He was speechless.

"William. I am begging you."

He looked into her eyes, once the stars by which he'd navigated his very life, now so weak, so lost. "I'll do it," he said softly, "I'll do it," though inwardly he remained uncertain.

She gripped his hand all the tighter.

"You didn't seem surprised to see me, by the way," said he. "All things considered."

She chuckled and subsequently coughed a little. "Because I knew you were not dead. You, my friend, will never die, but loom o'er the world like a great cloud, raining your brilliance upon the rest of us 'til we're drenched withal." Will made a face, as if he'd eaten something rotten, and Luce chuckled again. "You can't blame me," said she. "I've bedded too many poets—good, bad and indifferent. The urge to versify spreads like the clap."

Will beamed. "Now there's an apt analogy if ever I heard one."

He did not wait with her, heroically, until the end. Call him a coward; he certainly felt himself one. But he could not bear, could not have borne to see her go. She'd told him he could meet her son in the first-floor drawing room, and he'd fairly leapt at the chance to be out of her presence.

The only person in the room when Will arrived, however, was not what he'd expected. *Not yet old enough for a man, nor young enough for a boy; as a squash is before 'tis a peascod, or a cooling when 'tis almost an apple: 'tis with him in standing water, between boy and man.* This stranger was dressed like a young bravo, one of those fellows who wants to look wealthy, daring and dangerous, someone of great importance who'd brook no nonsense from anyone. As Will regarded him, the boy placed a hand on the hilt of the poniard at his belt.

"I'm sorry," said Will. "I was looking for someone. A boy?"

"There's no boys here," the other said, which came out, "they's nah boys heah," in true Southwark style.

Will cursed himself for a fool. Yes, the other had some African blood in him, but was much lighter-skinned than Luce, which only stood to reason, given her...profession.

"Ah," Will said awkwardly, "then perhaps *you're* Lucy's son?"

"I am. But no boy."

"Right. Of course. Well, my name's William," Will offered, raising his hand in greeting.

"And?"

Will coughed. Cleared his throat. "And...your mother thought perhaps you'd like to come...work for me." It was an odd proposal, he knew, in view of the fact he was dead and no longer had a career of his own, among other things.

The young man eyed him up and down, as if assessing the worth of his clothing, and said, "Doing?"

Oh, he was a hard one was Lucy's son. Suspicious, cynical, guarded. Will supposed it was to be expected of someone with his lot in life. Still, misanthropes did not make the best traveling companions. "Sailing to the New World, actually."

The young man's eyes lit up. "Are you serious?" he asked, suddenly excited. "America? You'd take me to America?"

"Well, yes, as my, er, employee…"

Suspicion crept into the boy's eyes and voice again. "What would I have to do? I'm…I'm not for men, if you get me."

Will nearly choked to death on his own tongue. Of course, the young man suspected his motives, living in whorehouse! "No, no!" he coughed out, "it's nothing like that!"

The other let loose a sigh of relief. "Thank God for that, then! But what *would* I be doing?"

Not having expected or prepared for this conversation, Will threw his arms out to either side. "I'm not sure just yet…carrying my bags? Looking out for pickpockets and highwaymen?"

The young man made a show of considering the offer, although it was obvious the idea of sailing to America thrilled him. "And, er, what's my pay?"

"You mean, in addition to transport to the New World?" Will thought for a moment. "Whatever I eat or drink, you'll eat or drink. Wherever I sleep, you'll sleep. I'll give you some coin on top of that, but how and where you'll spend it, the Lord alone knows. But…" Will paused for effect, "any return trip will be your own problem, as I mean to stay in Virginia."

"Deal!" the young man agreed. "And my name is Richard."

Will winced upon hearing Richard's name, but he took his hand and clasped it within his own. "I'll be back for you tomorrow, about this time. But let's meet out front, shall we?"

~ 6 ~

WHEN I WAS AT HOME,
I WAS IN A BETTER PLACE

Jamestown, May, 1619

The people of Jamestown were ever so much busier than those of Will's hometown. But then there was ever so much more to do. Still, he admired their tireless industry and their optimism, despite the few rough years at the settlement's beginning. The young village already had a church, as expected, but there was also a general store of sorts and even a brewery. Oh, there was only one variety of beer, but it served Will's turn, and he could always purchase more from home and have it shipped. Or he might learn to brew his own. He'd dreamed of it for so long; perhaps the time had finally come. On the other hand (or in addition), tobacco might be the thing in which to invest his time, money and energies. It had certainly exploded in popularity both here in Jamestown and back in London. Will might make a second fortune!

At any rate, the industrious people of Jamestown were hard at work expanding their little village, and it wouldn't be long 'til it was deemed a full-fledged city. New buildings—homes and more—were being built all the time, and it seemed to Will that his housing prospects, both short and long term, were better than his first sight of the Turnby place had given him to believe.

But he remained most intrigued by the much talked-of Jamieson homestead. In fact, he'd rented a horse and wagon to take himself, Xander and Margaret out to the property, along with a local councilman who would serve as a sort of agent on behalf of Jamestown, in the event Will chose to purchase the place. The locals avoided it as cursed or ill-omened, but Will saw that as an added surety of privacy, a commodity for which he'd have been willing to pay almost any price.

It was a warm, slightly muggy afternoon in mid-May when he and his companions set out. Xander took the horse's reigns, whilst Will and Margaret sat to either side of him. The agent from town, one Nicholas Koon, rode his own horse, in case he needed to return before Will was ready. Even now, more than a fortnight after arriving, Will's senses were overwhelmed with the heady aroma of American soil, of its trees and shrubs, and most particularly its flowers. The buzzing of insects was a constant presence, too, as were the endless chirps, whistles and calls of birds. Never, he mused, had he been anywhere so alive.

Which thought made him wonder again about the natives. The longer he went without seeing one, the more his imagination ran away with him and his anxiety grew. He recognized the mechanism, well enough. Time was, he'd have exorcised such thoughts through his craft. But there was no need for his services here. Here, he was a man like other men. Here, he would be known by what he could build, what he could plant.

"You're brooding," Margaret teased him.

"My apologies. Just wondering when we can expect to encounter these famous savages that live hereabouts."

Xander scowled in his direction, but Margaret indulged Will's fancy. "I am anxious to meet them as well, to examine other ways of being."

"Well," said Will, "I hope when we do first meet, they come not in numbers."

The would-be robber he'd killed aboard the George wasn't his first. Years earlier, he and some drunken companions had hit upon the notion of joining a foreign war as a means of making money and earning a bit of renown, of honor. Looking back, it might have been laughable if it hadn't proven so pathetic, so tragically pathetic. The war had been—as undoubtedly all war was—butchery. Mere butchery. And he'd been the only survivor amongst his group of staunch fellows. No, there was no honor to be had, no honor *in* honor. Ah, but he'd railed about it all before and to no avail.

But the dead man, now...he'd had friends, companions of his own. All fresh from Newgate prison, no doubt. Were they the vindictive sort? He wondered. Best to assume so and avoid any who'd been aboard with him. He could hardly afford hostilities with the locals *and* the Powhatans.

The "road" to the Jamieson place had been cleared by hand, by Master Jamieson himself and his neighbors. As such, it avoided obstacles that were too hard to move and instead unerringly chose the easiest path, sometimes winding well out of the way before eventually settling back in the desired direction. Will imagined a future in which this road was so well travelled that a team of laborers could be hired, along with oxen, to clear and pave it properly. Or perhaps the passage of thousands and thousands of feet would do that work naturally. In some ways, it would be a pity. The meadows, the glens, the creek-crossings and forest floor were all so enchanting that Will half-expected the Queen of the Fairies herself to come floating out from behind the nearest oak. Indeed, he had a difficult time convincing himself of the danger of these places, and yet it was towards the site of a past danger that he and his companions moved. The ruts of wagon wheels branched off to his right once and also to his left farther along, evidence that the Jamiesons had not lived in complete solitude, though neither home was visible from the road.

In time, Jamestown's agent announced, "Tis this one, here!" and gestured down a new set of wheel ruts climbing just over a small rise to his right. That done, he led the group forward with nary a backward glance. Cresting the little hill, Will saw a healthy forest clearing with a bit of meadow—man-made, perhaps—bounded by lovely trees and what looked to be a brook at the back. The house, simultaneously rustic and elegant, stood near the middle, some half-mile away, with a great, lone oak for company.

A butterfly flitted across Will's vision and, from thence, off into the wildflowers that grew seemingly everywhere one looked.

"Timber, fresh water, fertile land and more than enough room for the three of us," Will said quietly, so that only Margaret and Xander could hear.

"It's not too far from town?" Xander asked, skeptically.

Once they'd arrived to Mr. Koon's satisfaction, he dismounted, looped his horse's reins to a stump used for splitting logs, and said, "Here she be, and a beauty she is, too. We'd love to have her occupied."

"I'm sure," Will replied, as he offered a hand to Margaret, that she might get down easier. Xander, of course, fairly bounded from his seat and onto the grass.

"But," Koon sighed, "I'm guessing you've heard the stories..."

"The family who built this place was eaten by bears," said Will.

"Might be," said Koon, stuffing his pipe with fresh tobacco and sparking it alight. "Or it could be something else got 'em."

"Indians?" Xander asked.

Mr. Koon took a long, thoughtful puff. "The Powhatans covet copper, tools, trinkets 'n such. Whoever—or whatever— killed the Jamiesons didn't touch a thing of value. But they painted the insides with the family's innards. Took a crew of us a week to clean it." This speech, of course, brought about a lengthy and awkward pause. Finally, he said, "Discourage you, does it?"

Will snickered. "Your sales pitch needs some work, but, no, I'm not discouraged. I've seen more than my share of bloodshed. If the house be sound, the fireplace well-built, and yon creek be sweet to the taste, she'll serve our turn."

"May we see the inside?" Margaret asked, anxious, it seemed, to prevent Will from getting ahead of himself.

"O' course," Koon replied, taking another puff of his pipe.

"I believe I'll scout the grounds," Xander added.

Master Koon entered the home and immediately set about opening the shutters, to let some light into the place and freshen the air. As he talked, Will caught glimpses of Xander through the various shutters, making a slow circuit of the cottage. Will tried to imagine what his son was thinking in this moment, in an environment as far from the shops and alleys of Southwark as Virginia from the moon. It must have been like being dropped into a world where all the colors were different, the water, dry, and the air, solid. Xander would adapt, Will knew, in time. He was a bright young man and determined, too.

Koon said something, and Will's thoughts returned to the matter at hand.

The main room of the cottage was a large space, full of natural light, with a table big enough for six, an excellent fireplace, and an area for preparing meals. A ladder led to a loft where one or two might sleep and household goods might be stored. There was also a narrow hallway off to the right of the main room that led to the back of the cottage, where two smaller rooms were located. Beds occupied both rooms, and it seemed likely, to Will, they'd continue to do so, unless he replaced one with his own. It was the reed mat on the floor of the main room that he found most interesting, though.

"This is native work, I take it?" he asked of the agent.

The man looked down and considered the thing. "Oh, aye. These and corn are mostly what the savages give in trade, though you may see some meat from time to time. This one is meant to replace the former, what was stained with blood."

Will ignored this last and said, "Still, it's quite a piece, this."

"'Tis that. These Powhatans are clever. It don't do to underestimate them."

"I'll keep that in mind."

"See you do, friend. See you do. Now, as to this place…"

Ah, the haggling had begun. Will was many things, but a fine man of business was surely amongst the top two or three. He knew the people of Jamestown, and particularly its leaders, were anxious to have this land occupied, because it represented an outpost of sorts, a boundary, that if left neglected would cede territory back to the natives. There was also the composition of Will's party to consider. Prejudices being what they were, he imagined that neither Margaret nor Xander would ever be entirely welcome in town. And so, he felt he had some leverage in negotiations over price. Margaret, uncomfortable with potentially overhearing the details of Will's financial status, chose to rejoin Xander outside. It was, briefly, a rather tense discussion, but, in the end, Will was correct in his assumptions and was able to secure the home and its lands at what he deemed a bargain price.

When he emerged, smiling, from the cottage, his companions knew he had won the day.

"You look pleased with yourself," Margaret observed under her breath.

"And so I am!" said Will. "This purchase was the very last leg of our long journey from London. We are home, now—assuming you'll stay with us?"

Margaret laughed. "I shall. Where else would I find two such fascinating men for company?"

Xander shook his head, the way an exhausted parent does at a precocious child.

"And now?" Margaret asked.

Will gestured to the agent, who stood a respectful distance from the group. "We follow this good gentleman back to town, to finalize the agreement and to hire help in moving."

"But not that old man and his son, surely," Xander said.

Will beamed. "I think we can do better, now we know our way around a bit."

~ 7 ~

JOG ON, JOG ON, THE FOOTPATH WAY!

Jamestown, May, 1619

They were gathered near Jamestown's modest general store when two men with muskets approached the town's leader, Sir George Yeardly, in a hurried, breathless manner. After a few whispered comments, Yeardly drafted several more fellows and followed the first two towards the gates and beyond.

Will, Margaret and Xander exchanged looks of confusion and curiosity.

"I'll follow 'em," said Xander. "It's what I do."

"Yes, but…" Before Will could finish the sentence, Xander had slipped away. Will looked to Margaret, plaintively. "I meant to say, 'Yes, but not here, not in Virginia.' Don't know as the lad's got any experience in the woods."

"Not yet," was all Margaret offered in reassurance.

There wasn't much Will needed from the general store, but it was always good practice to double and triple check. One could never predict what little thing might prove the difference between eating and hunger, comfort and freezing, safety and death. He had purchased, with his new homestead, all of the tools that went with it, and so he ignored the spades, the axes, the twine. Instead, he bought some tobacco, a well-used deck of playing cards and an obscenely expensive spyglass that he was told was not for sale, but turned out to be so for the right price. He was also intrigued by a number of items manufactured by the natives—a variety of mats, bow and arrows, and small pots of powder.

"What's this, then?" Will asked the old woman tasked with running the store at the moment.

"That one?" she confirmed, pointing to the nearest pot. "Slippery Elm, I think. Powhatans use it for pain and such."

Will was intrigued. "Really? And the others?"

The woman sighed, as if her customer was working her harder than she'd planned. "That one," she pointed, "is meant for a sour stomach. The next is for a gentle sleep. The next is for ague…"

"I'll take the lot!" Will cut in. He'd had a secret fascination for all things alchemical for years, and here were substances largely unknown in London. Perhaps here, at last, was the secret to balancing one's humors, extending one's lifespan, or gaining other heretofore undreamt-of abilities. A man needed a hobby after all.

Margaret gamely played along, having comparatively little money of her own to contribute to the household, and helped Will load everything into their borrowed wagon. Several of the townsfolk had agreed to meet them at the Turnby place to aid in the transference of their belongings to the Jamieson house. It would take, Will estimated, a good three or four trips back and forth to get it all done, but the weather was fair, the day young, and spirits were high. Xander had not returned by the time the first load was ready to depart, so Will left a message with the locals that the young man could catch him on his return trip.

First things to go, of course, were Will's bed and his books, along with all his weapons, save the flintlock. That, he kept on his person the while, should the unexpected occur. A few of the townsfolk rode ahead, ostensibly to aid in the offloading, but in reality, Will suspected, out of curiosity.

As Will climbed onto the wagon bench next to Margaret, she cleared her throat.

"Before we make this arrangement official," she said, "I have a confession to make…"

Will said nothing, but sat up straighter all the same.

"I knew you…was *aware* of you, anyway…in your former life."

"Were you?"

Margaret gazed into her lap, remembering. "I was a member of Paul's Boys—one of your little eyases, I think you called us—and then later I played all the women for the Lord Admiral's Men. Eventually, I came to prefer living this way. But...I know you."

"It's just as well," Will sighed. "And I can't think of a better soul to witness my second life." With that, he flicked the reins and urged the horse forward—the same horse, he believed that had been attached to a different wagon when he'd first arrived in Jamestown.

"I must say," said Margaret, "that I'm relieved to hear you say so. I don't know what I would have done without your help thus far."

"I have been wondering what you had planned for yourself before meeting me."

"I was going to open a school for wayward girls, of course," Margaret beamed, coaxing a laugh from her friend. "Or, at the very least, indenture myself to some family needing a nanny or kitchen scullion."

"You'd make an excellent scullion, I'll wager!" Will exclaimed.

"Wouldn't I just?"

The two fell into an amiable, pleasant silence, which allowed the world around to intrude again, and Will observed there'd been hardly a moment in Jamestown when he hadn't heard the sound of hammering, sawing, or digging. Gunfire and the barking of dogs were also not uncommon, which thought made him wonder how he might acquire a dog of his own. He'd always wanted one, but the timing had never been convenient. Here in Virginia, it seemed not only convenient to own a dog, but prudent as well, for the silly beasts were privy to things, so they were. Privy to secrets, privy to warnings, privy to signs to which most men were oblivious.

"I think we need a dog," said Will.

"An excellent idea!" Margaret agreed. "Perhaps Xander can ask around...?"

"I'll broach the subject...if he ever returns."

He did, of course. On Will's last trip from town back to the Jamieson house, Xander appeared as if from nowhere and leapt onto the wagon bed, startling both Will and Margaret. As they rode along, Xander made his way forward, until he sat just behind Will.

"There's been another killing," he breathed.

"Of a settler?" Margaret asked quietly.

"They can't tell. Could be one o' the natives, but the body was ripped to pieces and the flesh was all gone."

"I still say it's wolves or a bear," Will insisted. "Are there lions in Virginia?"

"The men I overheard say it looked to have been done in a rage."

"And they're certain it's not the Powhatans..."

"Dead certain, if you'll pardon my saying so."

Will put a hand inside his vest and rested it on his flintlock. "Now entertain conjecture..." he muttered to himself. "Not a known animal. Not a native. Is there a madman in Jamestown?" he wondered aloud.

"'Faith, I hope not," said Margaret.

"They're planning a hunting party," said Xander.

"When?"

"Tonight," Xander replied.

Margaret was shocked. "At night?"

"So, they said."

"Well," said Will, "I won't join them. I'll be in my own home, enjoying a fine fire and a good pipe of Virginia tobacco. Still, this action smacks of desperation."

"What have we gotten ourselves into?" Margaret asked.

Xander put a hand on his poniard. "Nothing we can't get ourselves out of."

Will wished he had the boy's confidence.

The first night in their new home was uneventful and pleasantly so. There was much to do to arrange the furniture and other belongings to everyone's satisfaction, especially Will's. The cottage had few shelves and he'd not thought to purchase any in town, and so his books were carefully stacked atop their packing crates, against the wall.

It had taken all three of them to get Will's bed into the first room off the narrow hallway and remove the existing one, after which effort Xander said, "I hope never to lift that monster again."

"I'll agree with that!" Margaret added. "Though it's surely the finest bed in the New World."

Will snickered. "I should hope so. It cost enough."

"If you'll help me drag this other bed up into the loft, I'll sleep there," Xander said.

"A fine choice!"

"But where will Margaret sleep?" Xander wanted to know.

Without losing a beat, Will said, "She can sleep in my bed tonight, as a reward for all her labor. I'll just take the back bedroom..."

"Nonsense!" Margaret replied. "You bought this house and land, you own the bed, you'll sleep in it."

Will cleared this throat. "There's uh...there *is* room for more than one of us..."

Margaret and Will eyed each other for an uncomfortable season, before the lady said, "Didn't I once hear something about adversity or somesuch making for strange bedfellows?"

"Did you?" Will asked, all innocence. "Which side of the bed do you prefer?"

And that was that. Margaret claimed the side nearest the wall and Will, nearest the door. They shared the same bed from then on.

They stood, father and son, leaning upon the rail of the fence that surrounded the Jamieson garden and vegetable patch, and Will was reminded of the first time they'd stood thus, together, at the rail of the George as it pulled away from London. Will imagined the boy's face—a riot of emotions—was a fair reflection of his own, where anyone watching could see excitement, fear, regret and more. He had wanted to say something, then, to ease the lad's distress and promote his excitement, but the chasm between the two was as wide as the Thames itself. They had been strangers, after all, thrown together by necessity and a promise. Oh, Luce had claimed the boy was his own at parting, but Will's vanity had died with his hairline, so he had to accept the possibility that she'd been lying to him (again), manipulating him (again) by telling him what he wanted to hear (again). Oh, willing victim! Since the death of his natural son years earlier, he'd suffered from a vast emptiness, a sense of fatalistic futility that sometimes made even breathing seem a chore. But this little deceit of Luce's, if deceit it was, had given him hope. Too much, perhaps. For he'd come to believe it was so, come to see Xander as his own, and now the old fear that had once hung over his daughters, that they might join their brother in an early death, was again haunting Will's idle moments. Lord, William prayed, let this one reach manhood. Take me now, if needs must, but let him live.

Somehow, the days and weeks passed, and a kinship had begun to blossom. They had Luce in common, and Southwark, and, now, everything that had befallen them since leaving London.

~ 8 ~

THEIR SAVAGE EYES

Jamestown, May, 1619

Will was sitting on a small wooden bench just outside the cottage, enjoying his first pipe of the day, when the natives appeared at the far end of his field. He stopped breathing for a moment, still as a rabbit catching scent of the fox, and waited to see in which direction they were headed.

They were coming straight towards him.

Taking a long, slow inhalation, he reached out to locate his spyglass and flintlock on the bench to his right and carry the weapon back into his lap. "Margaret," he called softly. "Xander. We have company."

Xander was first through the open door. "That didn't take long," he said upon sighting their approaching visitors.

Margaret poked her head out next, curious. When she saw both men looking away, she followed their gaze until she, too, recognized the potential threat. "I'll fetch the axe, shall I?"

"Let's meet them outside here, and keep the door closed behind us," Will instructed. "Keep what little we own a secret for as long as we may."

The minutes dragged by as the trio awaited their visitors, who strode as casually in their direction as if they encountered one another every day. Will continued puffing on his pipe, and otherwise used the interlude to examine the day. It was cool and fresh. There was dew on the grass and sunlight on the leaves of nearby trees. It would be a fine day, after all, perhaps even a bit warm. If these were portents, omens, they spoke well of what was to come. But then, Will had seen many a man die in beautiful weather. There may have been, as he'd once maintained, a special providence in the fall of a sparrow, but a beautiful morning did not guarantee an equally lovely day, any more than an easy birth presaged an easy life.

In time, the natives drew within shouting distance, and Will saw that they matched the descriptions he'd heard in town. There were five of them, all men—tall, slim and well-muscled. Their heads were half-shaven, while the hair on the other halves grew long and straight. That hair was uniformly black. Their skin was a deep brown, though some of it was painted red or black. They were mostly naked, except for deerskin aprons across their loins, and they carried bows, arrows and spears, along with other items. Watching them, time seemed to slow down, to stretch in all directions for Will. A myriad of thoughts occurred to him then, though some so fleetingly that he hardly had time to register them. This instant, though, was unique in all history, whatever might come of it. This was what he'd come here for.

The natives' odor was perhaps the thing Will found most interesting, as they smelled much better than most Englishmen he'd met. There is always, amongst men, the heavy scent of sweat, but these people were also redolent of woodsmoke, of leaves, of soil and other things that savor of nature's dominion.

On instinct, Will chose not to rise from his bench as they approached, but remained where he was, in a posture of calm repose, flanked by his companions. Finally, the two groups stood face-to-face, spellbound by one another. Indeed, it was apparent the natives had never seen the like of either Xander, a fellow of African lineage, or Margaret, an erstwhile man in woman's apparel, and were as awestricken as if they'd heard a bear talking.

Slowly, carefully, one of the natives extended a hand towards Xander's face. The young man was about to swat that hand away, when Will said, "Now, now. They're just curious." Xander endured the stranger's touch begrudgingly.

Finally, the man in the center of the visitors said, "Friend," in heavily accented speech.

"Friend," Will repeated in a neutral tone, well aware that such overtures were often followed by demands.

The leader, as he seemed, turned to his fellows and uttered something, whereupon two of the others held up fresh game—a brace of rabbits and a beaver—and a woven basket of corn.

"Are we meant to take this?" Xander asked.

"More, I think," Will responded. "I believe we have to accept these gifts and then feed our guests."

"Inside?" Margaret wondered.

"Outside," said Will. "We'll use yon firepit."

Margaret nodded and slipped back into the cottage, not in retreat, Will understood, but to gather a few necessities. Will stood, despite a rather sober complaint from his left knee, and gestured towards the pit. The natives indicated that they understood, and walked over to make themselves comfortable. Two of them, though, took Xander by each arm, possessively, and escorted him thither. It would not be fair to say he looked frightened, but he was certainly not at ease, either.

Margaret reemerged with a shovel of smoldering coals in one hand and a bundle of kindling in the other and began to build a new fire in the pit. The natives watched her with great fascination, but she paid them little heed. She was used to being stared at; why should these men be any different?

"Xander," Will said, in attempt to extricate the young man from his smitten captors, "would you mind bringing some water?"

Try as he might, though, his new friends would not let him rise. "I can't," he groaned, plaintively.

"I'll do it," Margaret replied.

The natives gutted and skinned their game and cut it into pieces for roasting over the flames. They did not talk excessively amongst themselves, but with an economy Will found impressive. He'd spent the bulk of his life immersed in words and was learning to appreciate their absence. There was a peculiar freedom, a particular lack of burden, of obligation, of responsibility when dialogue ceased. And, too, there were all the other sounds that words drowned out, but which, when given voice, spoke most feelingly. It was intoxicating.

Sensing he might have missed something of import, Will brought his focus back into the small circle around the fast-growing fire. When his visitors did speak, Will made out the words "friend" or "friends," "stay," "meat," and a new one, "werowance." He knew enough French, Italian or Spanish to get by, but not one word, one syllable of this native tongue. Suddenly, in what amounted to an oration, one of the natives put an arm around Xander and said, "You come."

Xander, already on his guard, was immediately alarmed. "Oh no. No, no, no," he said. "Not me."

The native repeated himself with more authority. "You come."

Before things escalated into a full-blown dispute, Will jumped in, "Soon!" said he. "Soon."

Xander stared at him as if Will had slapped him across the face unexpectedly, but the native who'd used the word werowance said, "Soon. Good," and all the tension seemed to drain from the moment like wine from a broken cup. The meat was soon cooked and shared around and Xander, for all his reservations, ate as heartily as anyone. Margaret, on the other hand, was quite dainty throughout. As he looked at his companions and visitors, Will realized he was not only the most overweight of the group, but also the shortest. He could only console himself in the knowledge that he was the oldest, too, which in his mind excused some shortcomings, and the wealthiest, which dulled the bite of others.

In time, the fire burnt low, the meat was gone, and everyone rose to his feet. Xander and Margaret again received much attention, and Master Werowance offered Will a single arrow.

Will accepted the gift, bowed slightly, and said, "I thank you, friend," whereupon the natives turned and walked off into the wilderness.

"These, our actors," said Margaret, "As I foretold you, were all spirits, and are melted into air, into thin air."

Xander spat into the fire. "Are you two going to spout poetry at each other regularly? 'Cause if you are, I'm going to live in the woods."

Will and Margaret laughed, but it did raise the question, in

Will's mind, of what the younger man's long-term plans might be. Will had brought the lad along, just as he'd promised Luce. He'd even begun to have certain paternal feelings towards him. Was any more expected? Or possible? Certainly, Will could use the extra manpower around his new property, but what were Xander's goals? In a year or three, he might well be ready to learn a trade and make a home of his own.

For all his bluster, though, Xander did not move from the fire, and Will took advantage of the opportunity.

"There's safety in numbers, they say."

"Not if those numbers be hostile," Xander replied.

"Hmm," Will agreed. "But I was referring to Margaret and myself. You're welcome to stay here as long as you'd like. In sooth, I could use your help 'round here."

Xander snorted. "I can see you need the help. But I am nobody's boy," said he. "Not anymore."

"Of course not," Will answered. "You'd be an equal, a... company member, if will."

"I've got no skills in farming or carpentry."

"Nor I," said Will. "But we'll learn together."

Xander tossed a stick into the fire, said nothing for a while. Just when it seemed as if he'd finished talking altogether, he said, "I'm not going off with those natives. Not soon, not ever."

Will nodded. "I only said that to appease them. We'll hide you next time they visit."

"Then I'll stay," Xander said at last.

The truth, Will surmised, was that the young man had nowhere else to go. He'd been there himself, once upon a time.

Having at last encountered the natives and found them congenial, Will felt safe in making a walking tour of his property. Margaret agreed to accompany him, while Xander, perhaps still shaken by the werowance's interest, opted to stay inside the cottage, cleaning, tidying and arranging the disposition of the group's possessions.

The day continued to warm as the sun rose higher in the sky, and some of the morning's natural cacophony of bird and insect song subsided, allowing Will's ears to hear farther afield. For the most part, he heard nothing. And, upon reflection, he realized he'd never heard nothing before. London had been the very Capital of Noise, where a person was more likely to spot Athena strolling along the Thames than catch a moment of quiet. Stratford had been little better. And even aboard the George, there was always something to hear.

Hear. Here. Ear. Earth. Dearth. Mirth. Myrrh. Myrmidons.

How his mind wandered. A harbinger of second childishness?

Will decided to redirect his attention to all he could see.

The first thing he settled upon was a dandelion. He had read somewhere—perhaps in the writings of Captain John Smith—that dandelions did not exist in Virginia. And yet, here it was, single, solitary and bold as you please. How had it gotten here? Soon, he knew, there would be more, and then too many. Just as there would be more settlers, and then too many.

"We are God's dandelion seeds," he said aloud, "And His wind blows us where He will."

"I did not take you for a religious man," Margaret confessed.

"Oh, I believe in the Lord," Will said. "Just not the Church."

Margaret nodded as if this made all the sense in the world.

Will returned to his private musings.

He might have to fence in, to enclose his meadow if he meant to grow crops or raise livestock. It would not do to have deer or wolves invade his property. And then there was this thing, this nameless beast that had slaughtered the cottage's previous residents.

Perhaps he could purchase a small cannon somewhere. Or have one made for him. He'd noticed that Jamestown had several, but didn't imagine the counsel would be willing to part with any.

~ 9 ~

I Do Desire We May Be Better Strangers.

Jamestown, May, 1619

The heat of the day had passed and sunset was still an hour or more away when a knock sounded on the cottage door.

"Natives again?" Xander asked with a trace of panic in his voice.

"I doubt they knock. Margaret," Will said, "if you'll do the honors, I'll fetch my flintlock."

Once he was ready, Margaret opened the door, slowly, and with a shoulder behind it so as not to be overrun, in case of the worst. Beyond, stood some of the neighbors, a tall, stout fellow and his two sons, both of whom were younger than Xander, but not quite children.

"Evening," said the man.

"Greetings!" Will called from the center of the room. He'd tucked the flintlock into his belt, right in the center of his lower back.

"My name is Alvah, and these are my sons Henry and Jonathan. We're your nearest neighbors, across the way. We just wanted to see how you're settling in," the neighbor said.

"Excellent well," Will answered, "though we did have our first visit from the natives."

The other man nodded. "I thought as much. They're not especially harmful, though I've no faith in their promises."

"No?" Margaret asked.

"No," said Alvah. "They're like children. They want what

they want and will do almost anything to get it. Once they do, though, they quickly lose interest in it."

Will inwardly cringed at this characterization, as it was doubtful his neighbor or any of the other settlers knew enough about these Powhatans to make such an assessment. Enigmatic they may be, but fickle? He wanted more evidence.

"They tried to drag me off with them!" Xander exclaimed.

Alvah didn't even acknowledge that he'd spoken, but instead directed his next comment to Will. "Will you be needing a ride to church on Sunday?"

"I believe we'll have our own private services here at home," Will said flatly. "At least until we know our property is safe."

Alvah frowned at this news. "As you think best," he said without commitment. "We're just across the road if you change your mind come Sunday." With that, he gathered his sons—who were hard-pressed to tear their eyes from Margaret and Xander—and ushered them off towards their own land.

As she shut the door behind him, Margaret said, "I don't know why, but I don't care much for that man."

"Nor I," said Xander.

"Nor I," said Will. "But it's early yet. And we're a...*unique*... little triumvirate."

Over dinner, as was often the case, they discussed all the things that needed doing before any of them could feel fully secure in their new home. It was a long list and demanded prioritizing, so that comforts did not overtake necessities. For starters, there was the issue of food. Will—and, surprisingly, Margaret—had some little experience hunting, but Xander had none, except, he confessed, for skulking about the streets and alleys of Southwark after dark, on the heels of some client or other who needed watching. Will supposed they would have some success, but knew also that supposition fed no one reliably. He needed to purchase livestock and build—or have built—pens to contain it. He had to establish local trading partners within Jamestown. He wondered if any of the other settlers made cheese, smoked their own meats, milled cereal and the like. It could hardly be otherwise.

It was a long walk back to town to make this investigation, and Will knew his wretched feet and aching knee would punish him for days in the aftermath, but he could not ask or even allow Margaret or Xander to do it in his stead. He'd begun to get the very distinct impression from some of the locals that his little family was not welcome in Jamestown, and he was only tolerated for his money. And it would not be long, he understood, before money was worth far less than goods. Thus, he had to acquire and produce them. He would leave in the morning, he decided. He could always negotiate a ride back from town in the afternoon.

Now, the Jamiesons had previously established a plot for vegetables, and though it was wildly overgrown and in desperate need of watering and weeding, it was more than salvageable and might even provide in abundance with the right care and a little luck. Like anyone who'd grown up in the country, Will recognized much of what grew in the vegetable plot and could guess at what he did not. And, fortunately, there had been more Jamiesons than there were mouths in Will's little family, which suggested the current plantings were more than adequate. Margaret volunteered to tend the crops before Will even had to chance to ask. In addition, there were several chickens roaming about the place, the last members of the Jamieson clan. Will felt especially protective of them, since they'd survived the thing that had devoured their masters. He'd savor their eggs, of course, but spare the birds themselves. When Xander allowed that he'd like to learn to hunt, it seemed to the trio that they had the matter of future meals well in hand.

They were about to move on to the subject of security when a horrendous howl shattered the night, and their comfort along with it.

"That is no wolf," said Margaret, as tense and as rigid as an old maple.

"No," Will murmured, rising to double-check that the door was locked and barred.

Xander crossed to the fire and put one end of a lengthy log on the flames, leaving the other end resting on the floor, supposing it might come in handy as a burning club.

Anon, the howl sounded again, but farther off. Will exhaled as if he hadn't done so in days.

"I thought we might build a small palisade around the house, but I doubt we can do it on our own quickly enough." He sighed. "Yet another job I'll have to pay to have done, and the sooner the better."

Margaret and Xander were always silent on such issues, being, as they were, largely guests in the home Will had purchased and unable to contribute much more than labor. But he never seemed to resent them, never gave off the slightest hint he expected anything more than an honest effort in maintaining the place.

There came no third howl, and, once the fire had burnt down, everyone shuffled off to bed.

Will was awakened come morning by the sound of someone rattling the front door. "Who is it?" he called out from his bed.

"It's me!" Xander's voice answered. "I can't get the door open."

Next came the sound of Margaret's footsteps crossing the main room and reaching the door. There was a thud, then another, and then a great ripping noise. Will got to his feet and rushed to the bedroom door, that he might see the cause of all the racket.

Having heard him, Margaret and Xander turned in his direction.

"Someone threw tar all over the door, and it was stuck shut," Xander explained.

"Is it still hot?" Will asked.

Margaret held the palm of her hand an inch or two from the glossy, black substance. "Not hot, no, but warm."

Will walked to the door for a closer look. After a moment, he walked through it and outside, before turning back around and examining it from his new perspective. "Welcome to Virginia," he said wryly. This was a threat, he was certain, from the friends of the man he'd shot aboard the George. He supposed this kind of thing was as inevitable as it was completely unacceptable. What to do about it, though? He didn't imagine the governor or the town's council could be bothered with such a trivial complaint, destructive though it was. It was the implicit warning it embodied that worried him more. He pondered the tar. It not been painted on, but rather tossed at the cottage, in the general direction of the door, so that while most of it had landed in that one spot, it had also spattered over a wide area. Then, too, there was a sizable puddle near the threshold. He was amazed he hadn't gotten it all over his feet. Well, cleaning it off his home would take ages, but between himself, Margaret and Xander, he thought it could be done.

So much for his planned trip into town.

~ 10 ~

HOW FULL OF BRIARS
IS THIS WORKING-DAY WORLD!

Jamestown, May, 1619

The morning he chose was overcast and muggy, so that while the clouds kept the sun from making the day too hot, the humidity kept it from being too cool—an annoying state of affairs as far as Will was concerned. But it was decent walking weather, and he acknowledged that things could be worse.

As always, he carried his flintlock and daggers, along with his purse, a waterskin, and a stick that would serve as a cane. He wore a broad-brimmed hat that he wished he'd left back in the cottage, though he expected he might still have need of it if the sun chose to emerge later on.

It was a pleasant walk, at first, as these things always went. The trees were magnificent, the plants mysterious, and the various scents that greeted Will continued to bewitch him. If he'd ever been to a more pleasant-smelling land, he couldn't remember it. To pass the time, he tried listing off the aromas he could smell—pitch, soil, grasses, water, flowers. And then, a vague hint of putrescence, which seemed terribly out of place. With a hand on his flintlock, he gazed both left and right into the trees, saw nothing untoward. But now his curiosity warred with his growing unease and, for Will, the need to know always won out. He stepped off the trail to his left and into the trees, sniffing the air as he went, but within a few feet, he lost the scent. Returning to his original position, he repeated his actions on the right side of the trail. This time, the odor grew subtly stronger by the yard. Will glanced over his shoulder repeatedly, so as not to lose sight of the trail should he need to return in haste. The odor became a stink; the stink became a stench, and the stench became nigh onto unbearable, if all too familiar. It was the smell of rotting flesh, of corporeal corruption, that no soldier, no survivor of the plague would ever forget. Soon, there came the accompanying buzz of flies, scores of flies, and all that remained was to see *what* had died or been killed. Alas, what Will found offered no help, for at the base of a tree lay a pinkish-purplish mess of viscera. No organs were visible, for Will dared come no closer than fifteen or twenty feet, and so he deemed he'd discovered all he was like to know and began his retreat, looking about himself in rising panic and listening to his surroundings with every bit of concentration he could muster. Once he regained the path, he resumed his journey at an accelerated pace, hoping to put as much distance between himself and the rotting remains as possible.

But they tortured his imagination. They must have been related to that horrible howling he'd a few nights earlier. Who was doing the howling, though? The predator, or the prey? Where were the bones? The skull? Where was the skin? And as for the predator, clearly the town's 'hunt' had failed; why weren't the locals doing more to find and bring this thing down...or was this butchery the work of the natives?

Will pushed finding the answers to these questions to the top of his list of tasks once he arrived in Jamestown. He and his makeshift family had many needs, but surely not being torn to ribbons was first among them. Mercifully, his anxiety dissipated with every step towards town, making him wonder if his move to the Jamieson property hadn't been a bit premature. Death would find him, either way, but he preferred a peaceful to a violent end.

The rest of his walk was comparatively uneventful, although he did see a broad variety of birds, along with a squirrel or two and more butterflies than he could count. Yes, once the issue of this mysterious beast—if it was a beast—was solved, a man could live quite comfortably in Virginia.

His feet, predictably, complained loudly and constantly,

like a huswife with no milk for her children. A time there'd been when Will could've walked all the way from Stratford to London without feeling tired or sore. Now, even a trip to the jakes could be challenging sometimes.

Age. What was it good for, but punishing the old for the excesses of their youth? It was like buying on credit, or worse, borrowing from a friend. When the debt came due, it was often more burdensome than expected or imagined. And yet Will supposed even the virtuous suffered the ague. What, then, was the point in virtue? A promise of comfort after death?

It was the same old tired ground. And, sadly, he'd come no closer to understanding it. What he *had* gained, since coming to the New World, was a deeper and broader understanding of life. There *were*, in fact, more things in Heaven and Earth...

Few acknowledged him as he made his way into town. He got a wave or two and a couple of nods, but most of his new neighbors ignored his passage. *They'll not ignore my coin, though,* Will thought cynically. But unlike his Timon, he had Margaret and Xander to console him when and if his money was gone.

He made his way to the center of town, near the governor's home and the little store, where folks were wont to congregate between tasks. "Good morrow," he called to the nearest man, a gaunt and sober-looking fellow dressed in brown woolen pantaloons and a matching waistcoat.

"Aye," replied the man, as if Will's greeting had been self-evident.

"My name's Will Kemp."

"Tewkes," the other allowed begrudgingly. Casting about for allies, he gestured to another man standing nearby and said, "And this here's Robbins."

Will smiled. "Well met, Robbins."

"You must be the new owner of the Jamieson Place," Robbins observed. "Late of the Turnby Cottage."

"The same." This Robbins was more gregarious than Tewkes, it seemed, but both shared a certain standoffishness that Will found suspect. Perhaps it was to do with the natives, the Spanish threat, and this damned thing in the woods. If there was a thing. "A few nights ago," Will said, "we heard a terrible howling in the woods, and this morning, on my walk into town, I happened upon a grisly pile of offal."

Something passed between the two locals, and Will had no doubt it was fear.

"Did you, now?" asked Tewkes. "And whereabout was this?"

"Off the south side of the path, 'twixt here and my place. Maybe two or three miles hence."

Robbins scowled. "Did you think to mark the place?"

"You'll smell it clear enough as you draw nigh."

Tewkes nodded and spat into the dirt.

"I wouldn't think a bear would take a body and leave the guts," Will offered. "And bears don't howl."

"Oh?" said Tewkes. "You're a bear expert, are you?"

"I've been to a good many bear-baitings back in London. Too many."

"It's not a bear," Robbins butt in, earning a scolding sneer from Tewkes.

"Have we any idea what it *is* or what's being done about it?"

"Why don't you ask the governor, Sir George?" Tewkes said.

"Friends," said Will, tired of the locals' thinly-veiled hostility. "I know not how I have offended, but I apologize most heartily and take my leave." Perhaps he hadn't been foolish in moving so far out of town after all.

The governor was a man whose bearing and countenance reminded Will of many a friend and colleague back home. Although younger than Will by at least twenty years, he nevertheless had an aura of competence and command the older man found reassuring. And, unlike his fellow settlers, Sir George was not aloof, which pleased Will even more. Will happened upon the him in the center of town, sitting on a stool outside the town hall, poring over a map. He looked up when he saw Will's shadow approaching.

"Ah," said he, "Master Kemp, isn't it?"

Will doffed his hat and did a small bow. "The same. And what shall I call you, Governor, or Sir George?"

"Sir George is fine," said the other, standing. "You bought the Jamieson place."

"You're well informed."

Sir George pursed his lips at this, nodded. "Of necessity. What may I do for you?"

"I came upon a mess of offal on my way into town this morning, after hearing some terrible howling the other night. I should like to know more about these killings that include the previous owners of my land."

The governor glanced up at the sun as if he were estimating the hour and said, "As would I. It isn't the Powhatans, though, whatever the other settlers may have told you. I've seen Powhatan killings, and these new atrocities are nothing like."

"Some say a bear or wolves, but I can hardly credit those notions, either. I've seen what bears and wolves can do," Will said.

"And this offal you saw?"

"Intestines, viscera. But no body."

"Human?"

"I don't think so. Too much...volume...for a human victim."

"Well," Sir George sighed, "the best is, we're not this monster's only means of sustenance. Of course, this might be some perverse Spanish effort to frighten us all away."

"Do you think it likely?"

"I hold nothing likely or unlikely without further evidence, but I do not trust them. As for the dead? We've had only a few bodies, if a man could call 'em bodies, and we've had to put those in the ground, lest this heat spread contagion."

"I understand you hunted the beast the other night."

"And found nothing, not after hours of searching. It is beyond frustrating."

The conversation shifted to matters of less import. Eventually, both men went about their business, whereby Will was able to hire a few men to build a palisade around his new home and a fence around his property, more seeds for his garden, and place orders for a dog, a horse, and a quarter cask of liquor, should any or all of those things come available or arrive from England. He inquired, too, about tobacco seeds or starts and was warned that he'd be lucky to produce anything before autumn, but he remained undeterred. He also discovered that most of the local farmers grew hemp, as well, which had proven a profoundly useful crop for its diverse uses. Will had even smoked a particular variety back in Stratford and was not opposed to doing so again, should the opportunity arise.

In his search for a ride home, Will passed two men whose faces seemed familiar. One had a great hooked nose, and the other, by strange coincidence, seemed to be missing most of his, so that between the two, they possessed enough for two normal noses, but neither looked good with what he had. They must have been fellow passengers on the George and, judging by the naked hostility in their expressions, friends of the man he'd killed aboard. They were digging a hole in a field as Will approached and stopped when they saw him, gripping their shovels like axes or clubs. He'd no doubt they'd put him in that hole if not for the facts that it was broad daylight and there were other settlers around who might witness his murder. So, he'd come to the New World and immediately found enemies. And maybe these two were the cause of the general chill he felt when speaking with almost anyone else in town. Well, they bore watching.

It was getting late in the day when he finally convinced someone to bring him back to his homestead. It was again Master Koon, who'd helped him purchase the Jamieson property. This time, Will had to ride behind the man on his horse. It was not the ideal arrangement, but far better than walking in any case. Koon asked how Will was enjoying his new home and whether or not he'd had any encounters with the natives—'savages,' he called them—or seen any hint of the dreaded Spanish.

"I shared a meal with a small number of natives who came by to visit. As for the Spanish," Will said, "I have seen less than nothing. They seem more a bugbear meant to frighten small children than an actual danger to the colony. Has anyone, anywhere in Virginia, met or seen a single one of them?"

"By the time one sees them, it is often too late," the other countered.

Koon dropped Will off at the edge of his property, as sunset was approaching and the man had no desire to linger outdoors any longer than necessary. Will thanked him and began hobbling down the path towards his house, his knee and feet protesting with every step.

He still had several hundred steps to go when Margaret emerged from the cottage and came running towards him. It was almost as if a great bell or drum had sounded, so ominous was the moment, but Will held his tongue and endeavored to keep an open mind.

"They've taken him!" Margaret yelled as she came closer. There was no question of whom she was speaking.

A terrible, all-consuming panic seized Will then, and he pushed himself to walk faster and thus reached his still-running friend all the sooner. "Someone's taken Xander?" he said. "Who?"

"The Powhatans," Margaret answered, not breathing anywhere near as heavily as Will might have expected.

He looked about at the lengthening shadows and said, "Let's get inside, and then you can tell me all about it."

It was, for such a relatively short distance, one of the longest walks Will could remember, a distance measured not in feet but in fear. They made it, of course, long before the sun finally disappeared, but Will took nothing for granted.

After ensuring the door was barred and locked, he limped to his favorite chair and collapsed. Without being asked, Margaret poured them both a cup of wine and sat down nearby.

"Xander was out in the field, throwing his knife at a stump over and over, when they lured him away. They were smiling, talking softly and moving quite slowly. Xander threatened them with his knife, but there were too many—seven or eight in all. Eventually, they encircled him, and he could not run free."

Will drained his cup and asked, "Lured him away? Did he say anything?"

"Oh, yes," Margaret replied. "He told me to let you know."

"Damnation. It seems I chose the wrong day to go into town."

"I think they've been watching us, waiting for such a moment. If it hadn't been today, it would have happened some other day."

Will's chin sank onto his chest as he brooded on the matter.

"And it's too late in the day to go after him."

"We could get lost in the dark," Margaret agreed. "Or worse."

"I'll leave at sun up."

"*We'll* leave at sun up," Margaret corrected him.

"But the cottage..."

"Will be fine for a few hours, whereas Xander may not."

Will could not argue with that.

~ 11 ~

THOU, NATURE, ART MY GODDESS

Jamestown, May, 1619

His feet were no better in the morning. In fact, the first few steps were agonizing, but the pain subsided as Will walked about the cottage and got his blood flowing. However much they and his knee…and his gut…and his back bothered him, Will knew Xander's life might be in danger, and everything else seemed to fade into insignificance. While Margaret put together a light breakfast and packed lunch, Will gathered his weapons, including the axe. He hoped they wouldn't be necessary, but he was certain Xander hadn't gone of his own free will. He'd been taken with force, and force might be needed to retrieve him.

Outside the cottage, there was a good, strong breeze that promised pleasant weather. A small blessing, to be sure, but one that could well extend the time in which Will might search.

"Should we not ask our neighbors for help? Or send back to town?" Margaret asked when she emerged from the cottage.

"Certainly we should, but we've no time," Will answered. "The natives have already gotten a half-day's lead on us. And we've got to be indoors by nightfall."

Finding no weakness in his argument, Margaret said nothing in response, but instead shouldered her bag of supplies and glanced off into the forest.

"Off we go, then," said Will.

It was too easy to become distracted by Virginia's flora and fauna, and they crossed many a meadow and scaled many a hill that Will wished to explore further, perhaps even to claim for himself without really knowing why. He recalled a time as a boy when he'd gone to a local farm to pick berries. There were so many and they were so tantalizing that he could hardly resist picking more than he could carry or afford. It pained him to leave so many behind, even though he understood that the amount he'd already picked could not possibly be eaten before they went bad. Still, he wanted more. And this was how he'd come to feel about the New World. He wanted to see more, to own more and reason not the need!

But of course, Xander's rescue—if rescue was still possible— held precedence, not just for the young man's safety, but for Will's fear that Lucy's shade would haunt him for the rest of his days should her son die at the hands of his captors. And…Will cared for the lad. His kidnapping suggested these natives were hostile or at least dangerous. And then there was the ravenous animal that stalked these woods.

Will inhaled deeply and sighed. One thing at a time.

It wasn't long before he and Margaret reached the boundary of the settlers' territory and pressed on into the wilderness. The villagers' "road" was gone, but there remained game and footpaths through the undergrowth that Will assumed were known to and well-used by the Powhatans. How long had they lived in this area? Generations? Centuries? Or longer still? How had they gone so long without discovery by Europeans? And as they had, might not other races exist as yet undiscovered? Magellan's crew had sailed around the world, they said, but surely not seen every part of it.

Will stopped to drink from a waterskin and rest for a moment.

"What are you thinking about?" Margaret inquired.

"Everything and nothing. I apologize for being such dull company."

"Not at all!" said Margaret. "We need to keep our eyes and ears open certainly, but…maybe a little chatter will keep the bears away?"

"Bears!" Will chuckled. "As if we don't have enough to worry about."

After a pause, Margaret said, "Do you plan to write anymore?"

Will looked down at his feet, a frown on his lips. "I don't know. I don't believe so."

Margaret sighed. "Oh, it pains me to hear you say that."

"I once saw a man with a great, bright blue bird upon his arm," said Will after a lengthy silence. "It was a marvelous thing; it could talk, dance and do tricks. But I noticed after a while that its wings were clipped. It could never fly free, but was destined to serve its master forever, performing until the day it died. I would not be such a creature. I am more than my speeches, my songs, my tricks. Or at least I should like to be."

"And now that you've flown, are you happier?"

"This current dreadful business aside, this New World is a land of more wonders than people—quite the opposite of England, I think. If I *could* write…" Will trailed off. "But no, there's too much expectation."

"That is a topic with which I am all too familiar."

Will glanced up into Margaret's face. "I imagine you are," he said. "And now that *you've* flown?"

"We've been here but a brief time. We shall see."

The conversation dwindled off, and the search resumed in earnest. The pair saw evidence of animals in spoor, in tracks, even in the occasional molted fur, but of the natives, nothing. By midday, they'd walked for hours. Will's stride had become a pronounced limp, and try though he might to conceal it, Margaret missed nothing.

"Strong I may be," said she, "but I very much doubt I can carry you all the way back."

There was no point in dissembling, but Will was not ready to give up on the search just yet, either. "It looks worse than it feels. I can go a bit farther."

"And all the way back?"

"If needs must."

After a brief meal of apples, cheese and water, they pressed on. At one point, Will stopped and threw his waterskin to the ground in frustration. "They are all spirits!" he spat. "And are melted into air, into thin air.' Who knows, but what we say or write may prophesy our futures?"

Margaret sought the sun through the canopy of trees and said, "If we don't turn back now, we're like to be as lost as Xander. We've barely enough daylight left as it is."

Such was his mood, Will nearly confessed that he cared not, but he couldn't have Margaret's death or capture on his conscience, too. Without a word, he picked up his waterskin, turned about, and began the long trek back to his cottage. Margaret put a hand on his back in consolation, and Will heaved a bottomless sigh of anger and regret. For all their effort, they'd found no trace of Xander or his captors. Will could not help but fear the worst.

"The worst is not, so long as we can say 'This is the worst,'" he mumbled.

Margaret, who'd been lost in her own thoughts, said, "What?"

"I am trying to reassure myself that he may yet be found alive. But it is a daunting task."

"We've found no cast-off clothing, no blood, no body. Until occasion shows us otherwise, we must assume he's living still."

They did get lost once or twice on the way back, and that, combined with Will's aching feet and low morale, made the return trip longer than the initial search, all but ensuring they'd not get home before sunset. Birds and animals of the daytime gave way to those of night, and the wilderness all around became more hushed and intimate, so that Will and Margaret were loath to breathe too loudly, lest they call unwanted attention to themselves. They then spoke not in words, but in gestures and pressed onward, hand-in-hand, or arm-in-arm, or even hand-upon-shoulder. But they maintained contact with every step, for the thing they feared most was being separated in this forest, caught alone with the beast, the whatever-it-was that had killed the Jamiesons. Gone was any concern for Xander's well-being, replaced entirely with a desperate need for self-preservation. It's amazing what a little darkness will do. When at last they broke out into the open air of their own fields, they suddenly found the energy to run for the cottage. Will tripped and fell more than once, but didn't waste even a moment for embarrassment or anger; instead, he hauled himself up, confirmed that he was still in possession of all of his weapons—and his limbs—and resumed his lurching charge towards safety. Reaching the door, they barreled into their home and slammed the door shut behind themselves, locking and barring it before collapsing into a heap on the floor.

"Haven't…run like that…in years," Will gasped.

"Trying to catch a carriage?"

"No. Escaping an angry fellow whose wife I'd been romancing."

"Scoundrel!" Margaret laughed.

Will snored in response.

At some point during the night, Margaret had gotten Will off the floor and helped him into bed. When he woke up late the next morning, she had already made breakfast, put his gear away and done a number of household chores. After going outside to relieve himself, Will sat down by the table and poured a large cup of water from a pitcher Margaret had filled earlier.

When she came in, Margaret asked him how he was feeling.

"Like I fell down a flight of stairs, fell back up, and then fell back down. Twenty times." He drank his water and stared at a platter of dried meat, cheese and fruit before him. "I'll have to hire a group of locals to search for Xander. Men willing to stay in the wilds for a few nights, if need be. For a land with so little for sale, it's alarming how quickly the money goes."

"I have some coin," Margaret offered.

Will waved her off. "It won't be necessary. I've got the gold, and it'll do me no good in hell. I just felt a need to complain."

"Understood."

The truth was, Will wanted to drink himself into a stupor and sulk for days. He didn't expect to see his young charge alive again, which meant he had failed his Lucy, to say nothing of their son. This fantasy voyage to the New World had quickly become a nightmare. If he'd come by himself, perhaps, and pretended to be a simple farmer instead of a gentleman…

He wanted his pipe. He looked about, but didn't see it in any of the usual places. Margaret, who was already at work on a stew for the evening meal, hadn't seen it, either. Groaning, Will got to his feet and searched the bedroom and retraced his steps to the outhouse. As always, he scanned the trees, the field, the horizon when stepping outdoors. He savored the beauty of his surroundings, but also respected the danger they kept hidden as well.

No pipe.

He poked his head back indoors and said, "I'm going to search the field to the edge of the forest, in case I dropped my pipe during our run last evening."

"Shall I join you?"

"I'll be fine," he answered, "and you could certainly use a break from this surly old man."

She chuckled cheerfully in response, making him wonder, yet again, what he'd do without her good humor and supernatural patience. He remained deeply curious about her, too. She knew who he was, but he knew little of her—who she'd been at birth, why she'd chosen to leave, to flee England, what she hoped to accomplish in the New World. She'd dropped hints since setting sail, but, put together, they still didn't add up to a narrative that made sense. Coming to Virginia was no mere lark. It was, in some ways, an act of desperation. It was well past time she confided in Will completely.

The long grass of the field was furrowed where Margaret and he had come running back home the previous night. There were even places where small clearings had been made by Will's body when he'd fallen. Alas, none of these contained the lost pipe. Just as Will began calculating how far he'd be willing to search into the woods, he spied another furrow in the grass, crossing his path from north to south. From his current position, it might have been made by deer, by a neighbor, or even the natives; only closer inspection would reveal the truth.

But he was afraid; there was no point in denying it. If something sprang from the tall grass or charged from the tree line, he wouldn't be able to out-run it. Not after last night's effort. He glanced over his shoulder at his cottage in the distance and cursed himself for a fool: he'd forgotten his flintlock. As he stood there, breathing heavily, his pulse pounding, he realized that seconds had passed and he hadn't been killed. After a minute of this, he decided it was safe to approach the other tracks.

A rabbit bolted from cover and dashed across his path, causing Will to cry aloud, tumble over backwards and break wind to thunderous effect. He wanted to laugh, was dying to do so, but still didn't dare. As quickly as he could manage, he scrambled to his feet and scanned the trees. Nothing.

Like a rabbit himself, he crept carefully towards the tracks. He was no scout, no woodsman, but it seemed to him that whatever had passed this way had been large—a group of something, like deer or men, or a single, huge animal, like a bear. At least, that was what he'd told himself until he found the footprint.

It was enormous and distinctly misshapen. The grass made it difficult to see much detail; nevertheless, it pressed deeply into the ground beneath. Whatever had made the print must have weighed a great deal and been disturbingly large. Looking around, Will saw two other prints—neither of which was as clear or deep as this first—and immediately decided to make his way home will all reasonable haste.

A quarter of an hour later, he'd returned to the same spot with Margaret, his sword, and his pistol. Incredibly, Margaret did not share his panic.

"It's big, I'll grant you," said she. "But it also moves away from our path, instead of following it. If it had meant to attack us..."

"Yes," Will said. "though it's been in our home before."

Margaret surveyed the area as she said, "If this is the same one."

"Gods! Don't even suggest there are more of these things."

"You can't have one unless there were two beforehand. You *do know* how reproduction works?" Margaret winked at him.

Will laughed in spite of himself. "I confess to feeling rather unnerved at the moment. Xander's abduction gnaws at me constantly, like a worm in a corpse."

"There's a cheerful analogy to start our day!" Margaret extended her arm out of habit and Will took it.

"I'll have no commerce with cheer 'til Xander be found."

As Will was not up to the long walk back into town, Margaret went in his stead and took his sword with her. He offered his flintlock, but she would not allow him to remain home alone without it.

She hadn't been gone long when he began to regret her departure. He'd had no trouble ignoring his home's grisly history when Margaret and Xander had been present, but, now that he was alone, it was all he could think about. He was convinced this beast in the woods would return; the question was what Will might do to prepare.

He thought again of getting his hands on a small cannon, or having one made. But even a four-pound ball seemed too large for the job. What he needed was something between a musket and a cannon, firing perhaps a one-pound shot. That should be adequate to kill an elephant. He made a few sketches at the table, but his mind began to drift, and eventually he started experimenting with the various alchemical substances he'd acquired. Could he fashion his own explosive powders or elixirs? If so, he could make his own grenades, too.

After an hour of this, he became restless and stepped outside to sit in the shade and study the landscape. That, too, failed to occupy his thoughts or calm him for long. If only he had his pipe. Where was Xander right now, he wondered. Was he still alive? And where were the builders he'd hired? He hadn't been expecting them to follow him home, but surely they should have shown up by now? He thought next of the thing in the forest. Why hadn't the people of Jamestown put together another hunting party and gone after it 'til it was found? Rousted it from its lair in daylight and finished the thing? Or were there, in fact, more than one, as Margaret had suggested?

Nothing in Virginia was as he'd imagined or expected it to be. But then, wasn't that why he'd come? This gem he'd coveted had sharp edges; he'd have to proceed with the utmost care.

He went back inside to fetch a cup of wine. If he couldn't smoke, he could still drink himself stupid. As he reemerged from the cottage, however, he noticed the town's horse and wagon making their way down the path to his door. The same old man sat in his customary spot on the wagon's bench and the same boy, beside him. Will searched behind them, but they were alone.

Or almost so.

As they pulled up, the boy jumped down and ran to the back of the wagon.

"Your friend's had an accident," the old man told Will by way of introduction.

Will rushed to join the boy and saw a bloodied and beaten Margaret, lying on her side in the wagon bed, struggling to get up. "What happened to her?"

The old man chewed his lower lip. "I couldn't say. Fell down, maybe?"

Will snarled at the stupidity of this lie. "Where did you find her?"

"Behind the church."

With the boy's help, Will managed to get Margaret to her feet, though she needed support on both sides. "Behind the church," Will repeated. "She 'fell down' behind the church and—what?—blacked both her eyes, broke her nose, perhaps a few ribs into the bargain? Was she scaling the roof?"

"'Ow should I know?" the old man complained. "I brung 'er 'ere, didn't I?"

Margaret vomited into the dirt and nearly collapsed again.

"Help me get her inside?" Will asked the boy.

Ultimately, even the old man had to lend a hand in carrying her indoors and laying her down on the bed. That done, the boy returned Will's sword. A fat lot of good it had done her. Will offered her two saviors coin, but both refused. Still, he was generous with his thanks as they drove away. With Margaret now incapacitated and Xander missing, he could hardly afford to alienate anyone.

Going to Margaret's side, he gently urged her head up and helped her to drink the same cup of wine he'd meant for himself just minutes earlier. She managed to get it and keep it down, but the effort drained her, and in moments she lost consciousness.

Suddenly, Will felt more vulnerable than he had in ages, and more useless, as well. Had he brought his new friends to his remote homestead, only to lose them to violent fates? He grasped Margaret's right hand; there was life in her, yet. Slowly, tenderly, he began cleaning her injuries with a damp cloth, wiping away both dirt and blood, so that he could see the extent of the damage to her eyes, her nose, her mouth. There was blood in her hair, too, where she'd sustained a grievous blow to the side of her head. She needed a physician, badly, and Will could not imagine why she hadn't been taken to one in Jamestown. Surely, by now, the town had someone who served in that role. If she died because she'd been brought to him first… No. He wouldn't give in to such dark thoughts. She would live. He would do everything in his power to ensure it.

But now he faced an awkward decision: he would have to undress Margaret if he were to accurately assess her wounds. *If it were done when 'tis done, then twere well it were done quickly.* Nothing for it, but to do the thing. Peeling back the various layers of Margaret's clothing as carefully as possible, Will gasped when he saw her torso covered in great, blazing discolorations. Sure, she had broken ribs. Breathing must have been nearly as unpleasant as not breathing. What tipped the scales, then, he wondered? What kept her at it despite the difficulty, the pain?

He'd seen such struggles before and known many a soul to abandon the fight, including his siblings. *Why should a dog, a horse, a rat have life, and thou no breath at all?* There were mysteries to whose answers he was not and would never be privy, no matter how much he read or how far he traveled. There were things, fate told him, he was not meant to know, and this— perhaps even more than questions of life and death—galled him no end. *(Who) plucks off my beard and blows it in my face?*

He was too much in his own head, he knew—especially when Margaret's life hung in the balance. Yet, he had physic for it: a modest quantity of opium he'd gotten from an apothecary of dubious reputation. This treasure, he'd kept hidden in the bottom of one of his crates, wrapped in a sweaty old shirt of most fragrant character. He'd intended it for himself, if ever he contracted gangrene or syphilis or something equally horrible. But Margaret's need was greater.

Quickly, he fetched it from its hiding place and set a pot of water on the hob to boil. She'd have to drink the concoction, he decided. Smoking it, in her condition, was right out. He had no idea how much to boil, but reckoned he could give it to her a gulp at a time, spread out over several hours.

The task, like most, was easier in its conception than in practice, for he could not administer the stuff unless Margaret was conscious enough to drink and swallow it. It would have been a cruel irony to drown the poor woman whilst trying to save her. And so, it was hours before she was awake and alert enough to take her medicine. She tried to apologize, yes, she did, to explain what had befallen her, but Will would have none of it. Talking was wasted energy, and she would need every bit of it to heal. It was bad enough he'd lost Xander; he would die before letting Margaret do so.

Everything he'd planned to do that day went undone while he waited by Margaret's side, reading, thinking and worrying. It was almost amusing how his optimism about the New World had been dashed by hard reality. And it could still get worse. Nevertheless, he had seen wonders, and there were more to come.

Eventually, he settled into a chair at Margaret's bedside, content to wile away the time with his copy of *Holinshed's Chronicles*. He might be done writing, but there was always something to be learned from history. Two hours passed before he realized he was getting hungry. He put a hand on Margaret's forehead, checking for signs of fever, and exhaled with a great whoosh when he found none. It was early, yet, he knew, and internal injuries might still condemn her, but he took her relative peace and improved breathing as a good sign. Whether this was due to the opium he'd given her or the natural course of events, he'd no idea and didn't much care as long as she continued to rest. He would give her no more of the drug unless and until her condition worsened. Briefly, he eyed the cup he'd offered her, still half-full of liquid, and contemplated taking a sip or two himself. *What, courage man! What though care killed a cat, thou hast mettle enough in thee to kill care.* He stood, instead, and wandered into the main room to fetch some cheese and a pippin or two. And he wanted the wine he'd given Margaret, and so poured himself a cup to complete his meal. Thus equipped, he resumed his reading.

By late afternoon, his eyes rebelled against such hard usage and refused to focus on one word more. With a bittersweet sigh, he gently closed his book and set it onto the bed near Margaret. She opened her eyes ever-so-slightly at this and forced the faintest of smiles.

"If you were reading to me, I didn't hear a word of it," said she.

Embarrassed, Will answered, "I wish I'd thought to be so kind. Would you like me to read now?"

"No," Margaret breathed. "I don't think I could make sense of it. But I am thirsty."

Will poured her some water from a nearby pitcher and helped her to lift her head enough to drink, which she did as daintily as a cat at a river's edge.

"How are you feeling?" he asked.

"Mmmm," she said.

"And the pain?"

"Mmmm," she repeated, still offering a nascent smile.

When my love swears that she is made of truth,
I do believe her, though I know she lies.

"If it does get worse," Will said, "you will say so, though? I'll give you more of this special tea I've brewed."

But Margaret had fallen back asleep.

Best not to give her more, anyway, unless the situation was most dire. Will was no expert on opium, had only heard anecdotal stories of those who overindulged in the stuff, in fact, but he was wise enough to allow Margaret to dictate its further employment.

The shadows lengthened, and Will arose on creaking knees to assess the fire and rebuild it should that be necessary. During this task, he wished that Xander had been present, which, naturally, led him to reminisce about the young man's mother, Lucy.

~ 12 ~

THEN WILL I SWEAR BEAUTY HERSELF IS BLACK

London, 1600

He'd been the toast of London, had Will, when he first set eyes on Lucy, the very nonpareil of beauty. He had seen African women before, and those from many other far-flung lands, too. But Lucy's exotic perfection so outshone those others that she was like a diamond in a field of stones, a thing more bright, more precious, than all the rest combined, treasure enough to ransom a kingdom.

But not in London, where those of dark complexion were deemed less than those of light, just as those, in his profession, without a university degree were seen as rustic and uncouth imposters. Those University Shits—he understood them well, how they came o'er him with his wilder days, not measuring what use he made of them. If they looked down on *him*, what hope for Luce? She had small recourse but prostitution in all its forms, the sexual sort being most lucrative. But it also gave her power. Men came to her, begging, willing to pay almost any sum. Some, she broke. Others, she rendered broke. Those who might otherwise have fettered her in a life of servitude became her slaves and grateful they were while she seemed to care for them.

It was a windy, wet November evening when Will and his companions first stumbled through the door of the brothel where she worked, the brothel she would later own. Some of his friends had more conventional tastes, but Will was smitten the second he saw Lucy, so statuesque, so regal. No queen of ancient Egypt could compare.

Of course, she was no fool. She was not dazzled by Will's growing celebrity, nor even by his seeming wealth. If he sought her favor, he would damned well have to earn it. She laughed at and dismissed every sonnet he wrote for her and wouldn't even deign to read the epic poem he'd crafted in her honor.

"And what should I do with all this verse?" she challenged him one night. "Will it keep me warm come January? Can I sail upon it 'cross the Thames? Will it give me physic if I catch the flux?"

"But how else might a man win your heart?" Will demanded.

"Perchance it cannot be won. I know you too well, you men. Only too eager to sip our nectar, nay, to drink it all off, but nowhere to be found when our blossoms 'gin to wilt."

"I'll not deny that's true of many men, but..."

"And where's your wife, then, William?"

He was beaten, and he knew it. With as much dignity as he could muster, he rose from her bed and began to get dressed.

"And yet," Lucy said, "if one of your plays were to feature a man of my color in the lead, someone to show these Londoners that we're as brave, as brilliant, as noble a people...why then, I think you'd find me most...appreciative."

A fire came to Will's eyes then, as an idea began to take shape.

In the present, he scolded himself for his need to gild a past that needed no such frippery. His Luce had been divine. Had he been a man of greater courage...

But no. He'd been too jealous of the others in her thrall, and there had been many. And she, having no power in English society *except* her power over men, had not discouraged them. Will gave her an ultimatum; he might as well have cut off his own nose. He felt sorry for himself for a time, trying his best to forget that he had a wife of his own back in Stratford, raising their daughters and subsisting on whatever he sent her.

Yes, he was a blackguard, a knave. He was ashamed, even as he felt no need to change. What he would not, however, time would. *Have you not a moist eye, a dry hand, a yellow cheek, a white beard, a decreasing leg, an increasing belly? Is not your voice broken, your wind short, your chin double, your wit single, and every part about you blasted with antiquity?* He sighed. These morbid thoughts, he knew, would not make so bold with him with Xander here and Margaret on her feet and hale. He wanted distraction, and his books, at the moment, only reminded him of things he preferred to ignore.

It was going to be a long evening and longer night.

~ 13 ~

PURGE HIM OF THAT HUMOR!

Jamestown, May, 1619

His eyelids creaked open. His neck was stiff and sore. His back and shoulders felt as if he'd been stretched upon a rack. Methuselah himself never suffered such pains.

He'd fallen asleep in his chair at Margaret's side. *Sir, I am too old to learn!* Well, and what then? It was a mistake he'd pay for 'til early afternoon at the soonest. Cursing himself for a fool, he began the long effort to rise to his feet, when the sound of soft laughter greeted him.

Margaret was awake and watching him. "As you are old and reverend, you should be wise," quoth she.

"Bah!" Will snapped, though he was unable to keep a grin from his lips. Before he could summon a sufficient retort, she asked for water. Suddenly, Will had no difficulty rising to his feet and fetching the pitcher to refill Margaret's cup. He leaned in to help her hold it, but she told him, "I can manage." And so, she did.

"How are you feeling?" he asked.

Margaret coughed, having swallowed a bit too rapidly, and replied, "Like I was beaten by three or four stout fellows with staves."

"What happened, then?"

"I was beaten by three or four stout fellows with staves."

Will ground his teeth—ever an unwise decision for one with teeth like his, but he could not help himself. He loathed bullies and despised the intolerant. Surely, Margaret was beaten for the way she'd chosen to live her life, and what fucking business what that of any man's? Looking back at her, he could see she was still in considerable pain. He offered her more of his specialty, his *special tea*. The look in her eyes said she knew what the stuff was, or suspected, but she welcomed it all the same.

In a minute or two, she'd fallen asleep, leaving Will to consider the stuff in her cup. He sniffed it, swirled it around. In the end, his damned curiosity got the better of him and he took a sip, which shortly became two sips and then a rather large gulp. Still, he possessed enough self-control to set the cup down and push it away. Morning was not the best time to...

A warm lassitude, an almost sexual languor, spread through him. He forgot whatever-it-was he was meant to be doing. A little rest, though...

Something or someone was banging, somewhere. He rolled over like shadows creeping across a floor. Hello, Margaret! How had he gotten into bed? The banging receded into the distance. His beard was damp with drool.

Margaret mumbled something. Or maybe he had. His stomach rumbled.

He had to piss, wasn't sure he could make the chamber pot in the corner.

He slept.

The quality of light in his bedroom had changed substantially since he'd last considered it, which informed him that he needed to be up and about. Turning his head, he saw Margaret's bruised and battered face not eight inches from his own. He was in bed, yes, but couldn't recall the journey hither from the chair. A faint banging or chopping greeted his ears from somewhere beyond the cottage walls. He swung his legs 'round and placed his feet on the floor, marveling at the sensation. Every part of him seemed to be packed in sand, or to weigh ten times its normal weight. He wasn't certain he could move with haste even if his life depended upon it. But someone had to look after Margaret.

He moved into the other room, to tend or restart the fire. Once arrived, he didn't know what he was doing there, or how long he'd been there.

His fingernails needed trimming.

The fire had gone out, and getting it going again seemed a herculean task.

Why had he never written a play for Hercules? Now there was a worthy subject!

Somehow, he was too muddled to make sense of it and instead found himself gazing upon his new home from the darkness of the forest, watching a faint light creep through the fastened shutters. A great and seemingly boundless fury raged within him, and he grew terrified of himself.

He woke up in darkness on the stone apron in front of the fireplace, dust in his beard and ash on his cheek, fully and finally awake at last. He was hungry, thirsty and smelled of piss. Upon further examination, his breeches were damp. Well, at least he hadn't gone in bed. He needed to check in on Margaret, but first he had to build a fire.

Time was still playing him for a fool; the difference now was that he was aware of it. He could track the progress of his thoughts and actions and remember what he'd done and had yet to accomplish. Once the fire was burning to his satisfaction, Will stripped down and changed into different clothing. He supposed he could take his fouled breeches to the creek on the morrow. He then drank several cups of water and had a small meal of smoked meat and cheese and fixed the same for Margaret.

She roused much more easily than the last time he'd spoken to her, though she remained a broken wreck. He started her on water and stale bread, until it was clear she could handle more. Eventually, she worked her way up to cheese, but had no stomach for meat.

"I could make some pottage, I think," Will ventured.

"Do," said Margaret.

He might've expected some jape at his expense; the fact she did not offer one suggested she was still struggling to recover. He would know she was feeling on the mend, then, when her humor returned in force.

After she'd had her fill of bread and cheese, Will offered her more of his opium tea. This time, she declined. "I am sorely tempted," said she, "but then I'm sorely everything at this point.

But I fear I'd become dependent on the stuff." She didn't ask what the 'stuff' was; Will assumed she'd already figured it out on her own. "Has Xander returned?"

Whether she'd asked simply to change the subject, to take Will's focus off of her, or because she genuinely thought there might be a chance, Will did not know. And, truth be told, he resented the question. He'd enough to worry about without Xander's abduction and possible murder gnawing at his conscience. "He has not," Will said at last.

"Oh," said Margaret. "Would you read to me?"

Will arched an eyebrow at her. Having unintentionally darkened his mood, she was changing the subject again. "And the pottage?"

"Can wait. Read to me."

"What would you like?" Will asked. "Hollinshead? Ovid? Or perhaps you'd prefer *Malleus Malificarum*?"

"What is that last you mentioned?"

"*Malleus Malificarum*. It's about witches."

Margaret grimaced, as if she'd smelled something horrible. "Oh, no, I think we can do without further nightmares at the moment, don't you? How about one of your plays?"

"Very good," said Will. "No witches." He went into the main room, tossed another log on the fire, and returned with a large tome. "The Tragedy of Macbeth," said he. "Act One, Scene One."

Margaret struggled to stifle a laugh and it pained her. "You're a terrible one, Master *Kemp*. A right devil!"

"A right devil, perhaps, but not *The White Devil*. That's Webster's fault."

The banging returned with the sunlight, but this time, Will knew it for what it was: someone was building something in the fields outside his cottage. The woodworkers had arrived at last. Or he'd recognized them at last.

He rolled to his left and surveyed Margaret, who cracked her eyelids at his movement.

"Progress?"

"Always. It's only a question of direction: toward recovery or the grave."

"You should have been a poet," Will smiled.

"And who says I'm not?"

"Well, then," Will said, "you may read to *me* tonight!"

As he got older, Will discovered that he could not remember all the tasks he meant to accomplish on a given day unless he took a few moments beforehand to write them all down. Or it might have been that failing to complete these chores was simply more consequential at this stage in life. The once-endless expanse of tomorrows in which to get things done had dwindled, noticeably, to a feeble trickle, like piss from an old man's bladder.

When they'd been boys, Will and his friends had hung about the pageant wagons like flies on rotten fruit, forcing the players to shew them away before any work could be done. Oh, but how they'd loved the mystery plays, those boys, especially the one about the shepherds at the birth of Christ. As the boys got older, they earned a few pennies helping the performers set up and strike their wagons. On one such occasion, Will had pocketed a sheaf of papers that turned out to be some actor's script. In time, mere watchingor assisting the actors was not enough for the lads, and they fell to creating parodies of their favorite—and especially *least* favorite—plays. Here, at last, was somethingWill was especially good at, to the point that his friends stopped writing anythingof their own for fear of looking foolish by comparison, and instead opted to perform in these shows. As a side diversion, the gang devised a number of outlandish schemes to separate more visiting actors from their scripts in order to feed Will's ever-growing appetite for examples. They pilfered foul papers, actors' roles, books and even a ledger. His fellows had expected Will to be disappointed with that last and, well, he surprised 'em, for he found the details of the company's finances every bit as enthralling as its dramas.*It was possible to make money doing this?*

Inevitably, the other boys lost interest as they grew into young men. Women were more alluring and labor more profitable. Will managed to conscript his brothers into his machinations for a time, but even they were unable to keep up with their older brother's inspiration and enthusiasm where the crafting of plays was concerned…

And where had that inspiration and enthusiasm gone in his age? Had he been born with a finite quantity which, once spent, was as gone as last season's raspberries? Or might it not be more like atrophied muscles that simply wanted exercise before they could return to their former power? Or was there some other cause?

It was difficult to pick up a quill without being inundated with memories of the things he used to be able to do and create with such an instrument. But then, he used to be able to run, as well, and see his own knees from a standing position. Sometimes, his unused, atrophied talent was like a missing limb, forever beckoning him to do things of which he was no longer capable…or willing. This notion put him in mind of an old acquaintance, Jonathan Meeks, who'd lost a leg to disease—though the surgery hadn't abated the nasty, noisome sores upon his stump—and hobbled about so badly that everyone called him Swift. Swift was forever bellyaching about the feats he used to accomplish, when whole, to the initial amusement and eventual annoyance of anyone within earshot. He was an object lesson in abject lesions.

With a sigh, Will considered his quill again.

One afternoon, whilst checking on Margaret's progress, he caught her weeping in bed. She turned as he came in, and he noticed her beard stubble for the first time. Of course! She could hardly attend to her appearance whilst convalescing.

"Don't look at me!" she cried out, "I must be a frightful sight!"

With her blackened eyes, swollen nose and her equally swollen and bruised jaw, she *was* rather a fright.

"Not at all!" Will lied. "No worse than expected, given the abuse you've suffered."

"You're a terrible liar," Margaret replied. "I'm a gorgon, I know. Medusa herself."

Will reached out and placed a reassuring hand on her shoulder. "And yet, I have not turned to stone!"

"You're just lazy."

Give the woman credit: she'd not lost her sense of humor. "How may I help you?" he asked.

"Would you fetch my velvet bag—the wine-colored one? It's got all my face paints and such."

It was no trouble at all to grant her request, but, once she had the items she required, she discovered her hands were too shaky to use them and resumed her weeping.

Will sat beside her on the bed and said, "Don't you worry, my friend. I've done this task a time or two myself. If you'll allow it, I think I can set you aright."

Margaret wept harder still, but nodded in the affirmative all the same.

Carefully, Will upended the contents of Margaret's bag onto the bed and studied them for a moment. Selecting her razor, he said, "I think we'll start with a shave." She began to protest, but he stopped her. "Tut tut!" said he, "I'll be as gentle as an angel's breath. Besides, methinks you've grown marvelous hairy about the face."

She started to laugh again despite her tears, but even that proved too painful and she groaned to an immediate stop.

"No jesting, then," said Will. "I think we'll start with a little light cleaning of the canvas, though." Again, he left Margaret's side to fetch water and a suitable cloth. With soft, almost caressing strokes, he wiped and dabbed at her face, careful to avoid the worst of her bruises.

"You've hazel eyes," Margaret sniffed.

"Two of them, yes."

"And such long lashes! I'm jealous."

"Please! Next you'll praise my nose."

Margaret winced as Will touched a particularly tender spot. He pulled his hand back as if he'd been burnt, and she smiled at his reaction. "Why are you doing this?"

"Because you cannot?"

"No, I mean allowing me to live here, in your home."

Will daubed at her lips with his dampened cloth, perhaps to clean them or maybe to stop her talking. "I can think of a thousand reasons for and not one against. But, if you insist on an answer, a man needs company in his age. And what better company than someone who knows the theater, books, music…? You have the soul of an artist."

"But I was a stranger."

"Nonsense!" Will said. "You were an actor, and if all the world's a stage, that makes us members o' the same company."

"We few, we happy few…"

"Mistress, have you conned *all* my works?"

"Just the best ones."

Feigning a look of extreme umbrage, Will asked, "Do you mean to suggest they're not all equally brilliant?"

"Well, your *Henry VIII*…"

Will rose to his feet. "I must needs heat this cloth for shaving, if you wish to keep those lovely cheeks."

Again, Margaret struggled not to laugh as Will left the room. When he returned, he gently draped the now fully-wet cloth across her face. "I hope it isn't too hot."

It was, but Margaret did not complain beyond a sharp intake of breath. In seconds, she felt better and, in a few minutes, Will was ready to begin shaving.

Just as he laid the razor against her cheek, however, he paused, saying, "The irony in being shaved by a man with a full beard is only to be surpassed, I suppose, by the trepidation such thoughts provoke. Nevertheless, good my mouse of virtue, I shall treat your skin as if it were my own."

"Better, I hope."

He was aware, as he worked, that her eyes never left his face. He couldn't recall the last time he'd been subject to such scrutiny. Conversely, he knew that he was finally, truly seeing her, too. Little by little, he removed the stubble from her cheeks, chin and jaw, restoring the oh-so-smooth skin beneath, as if it had never been otherwise. Occasionally, their eyes connected and then one or the other of them looked away, like young lovers in their first dance. Would they share a sonnet now? He hoped not. He was woefully out of the habit. When the silence became unbearable, he feared what he might hear upon the other side and so preemptively filled it with talk.

"Where did you sleep on the ship?"

"Ah, the George. The ladies—what few there were—would not have me, and I would not have the men. I slept in a closet with old sails and odd bits of canvas."

Will shook his head. "If I'd known you then, I'd have invited you into our little quarters."

"I survived."

"Why, so you did!" Will reapplied the damp cloth, wiping away any last bits of stubble. "The canvas is prepared, and now for the painting."

Margaret smiled and stayed his hand. "I thought you disapproved of women's face painting."

"Yours is a special case, my sweeting." The truth was, it was both relaxing and nostalgic, in its way, to revisit this act he'd done hundreds of times in his younger years. And it was something of an intellectual and artistic challenge to minimize Margaret's bruises, to conceal the lines age had written on her brow, to accentuate her feminine qualities. When he was done, he handed Margaret her hand mirror. She was both curious and fearful of what she might see, but, once she looked, she broke into a broad smile.

"You've made me look like Cleopatra!" she complained, even as she admired herself again.

"The lady doth protest too much, methinks."

"Oh, aye, but I am no queen!"

"You are *my* queen," Will countered with a roguish grin.

And whether or not his painting flattered her, he had lifted her spirits and so his own.

~ 14 ~

A NEST OF TRAITORS!

Jamestown, June, 1619

A crew of six men was busy constructing a palisade to encircle the cottage, high enough that it could not easily be scaled and far enough from the door that it would not block too much light throughout the day, exactly as Will had specified. He made the rounds, greeted each of the workers, and showered them with encouragement and praise. Xander's abduction and Margaret's beating were clear evidence that a man needed allies in the New World. Allies, a fortified wall, and guns.

Give Virginia the first touch in this duel; he would still win the match.

One of the men, Will saw, avoided looking at him and even turned away when Will tried to catch his eye. It didn't take much imagination to deduce this was one of the fellows who'd attacked Margaret. If only she were able to get up on her feet and identify him. Well, it would be simple enough to lure the man inside the cottage when it came time to pay the men for their work. And then...? That part of the plot was still unclear. Given time, Will knew, he'd figure something out. He always had before.

The crew left well before sunset, wisely. The creature in the forest was not far from their minds, Will knew. Nor was it far from his. But during daylight hours, he let other worries take center stage—Margaret's recovery, Xander's absence, preparing his new home for autumn and then winter. *To everything there is a season*, and the beast's season was nighttime. Or at least that's how Will wished it to be. He could hardly countenance such a menace 'round the clock.

As evening approached, however, he could focus on little else. Would his door and the shutters at his window hold until the palisade was finished? When and where might he get his hands on that small cannon he now desperately wished to purchase? He stoked the fire and pushed his heaviest furniture in front of the door. He checked to see that his musket was loaded and ready and did the same with his flintlock. He sharpened the edge on his sword—much good it had done Margaret!—and his knives. But the more he prepared, the more he felt he was utterly unprepared. He thought of prayer, but he'd never been a praying man, and when he'd tried, yes, his words had flown up whilst his thoughts had in fact remained below, and only damnation remained in the sequel.

He needed other methods, other means of self-defense. And, as it was a beast he fought and not a man—or so he believed— he was not bound by laws of civility. Caltrops came to mind. And poison. Tricks and traps for every possibility. The folks in Jamestown proper were no doubt protected by their numbers. But out here in the wilderness...

Will looked in on Margaret, did a few chores around the cottage, and then returned to his alchemical studies.

A week passed, during which time, Margaret improved to the point that a physician was now unnecessary. She was able to hobble around the cottage and perform many small tasks on her own, and Will was only too happy to let her. Food was becoming an issue, however. Their store of staples remained good, but items like bread, cheese and meat were beginning to run out. Margaret claimed she could make bread, but it was clear a trip into town was warranted as soon as she was strong enough to fend for herself for a half-day or so. More, Will was nervous about leaving her alone with the work crew outside, a crew that contained, he believed, at least one of her assailants.

Towards the end of another day, Will stepped outside to survey the men's work. They'd completed the palisade in front of the house and along its two sides, and only the back remained to finish. Will stalked the perimeter with his flintlock in his belt, considering the craftsmanship and strength of the structure. Already, the thing had given him confidence. Already, he felt…

An agonizing pain lanced through his left shoulder from behind, followed by a line of fire across his ribs on the opposite side. An instant later, he heard a loud thud and spied an arrow, newly stuck into the side of the cottage. Will spun, taking an arrow in the left forearm and fired his pistol into the tall grass near the forest. Before he hit the ground himself, he heard a loud scream of pain, which brought a brief smile to his lips. Rushing to reload his pistol, his own labored breathing roared in his ears, and his heartbeat throbbed behind his eyes. More arrows were coming, he was certain. Arrows and then spears and, finally, clubs.

Margaret's voice called out to him from the front side of the cottage. While he was relieved that she was aware something was amiss, he did not want her to sustain any further injuries, and so he kept quiet, peering eastward into the trees. Is this how it ends? He thought he heard the grunts and subdued groaning of someone grievously hurt, but trying to keep his position a secret. There were words exchanged, also, but too low and faint to be understood.

"Will!" Margaret gasped. Though she approached from behind, he could well guess the expression on her face. "Bastards!" she exclaimed. And, "Don't move; I'll help you."

Again, he wanted to warn her away, but he knew it was futile. Besides, he lacked the strength. It was astounding how pain weakened a body.

She knelt down to him, holding the wood axe in one hand and a flaming brand from the fire in the other. In the fading light, her more masculine attributes were pronounced, and her anger, palpable. She handed the brand to Will and, with her free hand, helped him to his feet. It was excruciating for both of them, but neither complained. All that mattered was getting back inside and barring the door. The scent of blood was now in the air, and night was coming.

It was, perhaps, a journey of some thirty or forty paces from the spot where Will had fallen to the steps of his cottage, but it seemed to him as long as that from London to Jamestown. He feared collapsing at any moment and pulling Margaret down with him. He feared pursuit. He feared exacerbating Margaret's own injuries. Most of all, he feared the monster in the forest, all of which was too much fear for anyone.

Once safely ensconced in his bed, the rest of the night passed in a sort of fever dream for Will. Margaret plied him with lots of wine, but never, he noticed, his opium tea. It was just as well. He could get lost in the stuff, never to emerge again.

A clattering noise roused him from sleep, followed by a sudden brightness, which told Will that Margaret had opened the shutters. Instinctively, he rolled away from the light, only to aggravate his wounds. "Foh!" he coughed. "This bed needs a freshening."

"And no wonder!" Margaret's disembodied voice responded. "One or the other of us has been sleeping in it for days and nights on end."

He struggled to rise into a sitting position, but his friend's strong hands held him down. And there she was, looming over him.

"We've had rather a rough start, here in this New World," said she.

"Mmm," Will grunted in agreement. But as he would brook no talk of returning to England, he quickly moved on to other matters. "I take it you've seen my wounds? How do they look?"

Margaret sat next to him. "Not so deep as a well, nor so wide as a church door..."

"But surely not fatal?"

She laughed, dismissively. "You're made of sturdier stuff, sure. Though I do think we should get you into town for further treatment."

Will spent a good minute just listening to himself breathe. "Did you keep the arrow, perchance?"

"Of course."

"Those weren't savages attacked me. At least, not the native sort."

"No?" Margaret asked.

"No. These were the same villains who waylaid you—one

or two of the ones working on our palisade."

She turned towards him. "What makes you think so?"

"First, I suspect the Powhatans are better archers. Second, one of the men on the crew has refused to meet my gaze. I smell conspiracy, or something very near it."

"Or maybe your laundry needs washing..."

He chortled, wincing at the resultant pain. "And how are you recovering?" he asked.

"My sides are still sore, and it hurts to smile, but I'll live. In another day or two, we might walk into town together."

"I'll be ready," said Will.

~ 15 ~

AND BONNY SWEET ROBIN IS ALL MY JOY

Jamestown, June, 1619

William came in from the yard one afternoon to find the ever-mending Margaret reading his copy of Holinshead, and a sudden wave of sadness washed over him, for he understood in an instant that it wasn't the book, really, but what he'd hidden within it that she'd been perusing, which, in turn, reminded him of things he'd been struggling to avoid. That she looked up, guiltily, confirmed his fears. With a deep sigh, he tossed his hat on a nearby chair and shuffled off to his bedroom to lie down. When this mood was upon him, everything seemed a chore; even breathing became exhausting.

He heard Margaret's voice before he saw her.

"I am sorry," she said. "I was feeling a bit useless, looking for something to do, and I thought I'd read one of your books. If I'd known…"

"This would have happened sooner or later," Will said without opening his eyes. "Better now, I suppose."

"These sonnets…"

"Trash."

"They are not so bad."

"Rough sketches, at best."

"Then you'll finish them someday?" Margaret asked.

"No," said Will, finally opening his eyes to her. "I have found at last the limit of my talent, the one thing I cannot express with mere words. Were I William Byrd, perhaps, I might compose a melody sufficient to the task. But I cannot capture what must be said through words alone."

"I think you have," Margaret protested. "You've stirred something in me, at all events. I had no idea…"

"But we've all of us lost someone, haven't we? I would not be precious or maudlin. Everyone suffers; there is nothing special about my case."

"That is just the point," said Margaret. "I read of your loss and remember my own, and know that I am not alone in my grief." Will lapsed into silence for a time, and Margaret asked, "May I read one aloud?"

"I'd rather you didn't. They're cumbersome, clumsy, an embarrassment. When I wrote for Southampton, the words flowed so easily, it was as if my quill could barely keep pace with my thoughts. For these, I was constipated and have struggled mightily to produce only shit."

"Tush! They are an excellent beginning. A framework, if you will." Without arguing for another second, Margaret began to read.

> O, Fate, thou crueler thing than winter's bite,
> Than ague, age or penury can tell—
> What didst my child to thee to earn thy spite,
> Or what have I, that thou send'st me to hell?
> Why dost thou wink at murderers and thieves,
> Impart no justice to the worst of men?
> It matters little what the throng believes,
> Thy whims defy all those of mortal ken.
> My son, the hope and future of my name
> Thou tookst, whilst those of other men endure
> Unconscious of their fortune in the same.
> Whilst my boy rots, his fellows all mature.
> If ere I wrong'd thee, I do not repent
> For nothing merits this, my punishment.

"Why did you choose that one?" Will said. "'Tis too full of self-pity and does little honor to my son."

"It was on top. Would you prefer another?"

"No."
She read another.

I curse that ash that ashes made of thee,
From whose fell branches thou didst slip and fall
Not like a leaf that dying, flutters free,
But more a stone, to bruise the earth withal.
What was't about that tree that drew thee hence?
Was't Heaven, or mere escape that lured thee so?
Didst thou sustain some hurt, some cruel offense,
Or was it simply done for youthful show?
Whate'er thy reason, reason hath no balm
To heal my wounds, nor cannot tell
A world that stands amazed by my calm
'Twas I, in grief, that perished when you fell.
In climbing, thou didst fall beyond my joy,
In falling, didst ascend, my heav'nly boy.

Margaret lowered herself onto the bed, sitting beside Will's shoulder. "Tell me what happened, here."

Will closed his eyes again, against oncoming tears. "There isn't much to tell. He fell from a tree and landed poorly. I was in London."

"And you believe that if you'd been home, things would have turned out differently?"

"I do not."

"I'm glad to hear it, because you might have been in the kitchen, in the garden, in the tavern, and he'd still have fallen."

"Everyone can master a grief but he that has it."

"Will!" Margaret nearly shouted in frustration. "Not every comment requires a clever retort." After a moment of silence, she continued. "Loved-ones die, marriages fail, roofs leak, and dogs get fleas. We are, all of us, bound together by experience. This, you know."

"The pain of loss, though, is so damnably persistent," Will answered. "An injury that never heals, but with death."

"That's not healing, that's oblivion, to which we're all headed in due course."

Sweet, merciful silence descended upon the cottage for a while, and then, in a soft, vulnerable voice, Will said, "He was my silly little man, my own." Tears followed, gently, slowly, and led him off to sleep.

~ 16 ~

SOME SWEET OBLIVIOUS ANTIDOTE

Jamestown, June, 1619

He felt every one of his fifty-five years. His injured shoulder had stiffened considerably—a worrying sign—and his left forearm still throbbed, making it difficult to grip anything with his left hand. On his right side, a scabbed line traced the path of an arrow he'd narrowly escaped. These things, combined with the usual aches and pains he felt in his gut, knees and feet made walking especially challenging. But he was a stubborn fellow, and would not give his enemies the satisfaction of his absence from town. There was just one problem: if Margaret came with him to town, their home would be left unattended and thus vulnerable to ransacking by either the men who'd attacked him and Margaret, by curious natives, or both. Much as he liked his new companion—and from heartstring he loved the lovely bully—his books were the one thing without which he simply could not, would not endure.

"Only one of us can go, I'm afraid," he told Margaret.

She nodded as if this was self-evident and said, "Then it shall be me."

"But…"

"And I'll take your pistol."

"But…"

"None of that. Everyone in the colony knows you've got it; they won't expect it on me, and if any of them are unwise enough to try me again, well, there'll be at least one new grave in Jamestown."

"And what shall I do?"

Margaret threw up her hands. "Work on your potions? Write something new? Heaven forbid you should sweep!"

"You sound like a hussif."

"Then be like I am."

There were always chores to be done, tasks to be performed. The Jamiesons, for instance, had kept chickens, and Will cherished their eggs, which needed to be gathered frequently. And wood had to be chopped, water hauled from the creek, such diverse greens to be gathered as the local environment allowed. From sundown to dawn, however, there was nothing to do but converse, read, and relax.

For a while, he amused himself with his alchemical experiments, taking great care to chronicle every step, every detail of everything he attempted. When several hours of effort produced nothing of note, he became frustrated and retired to his favorite chair by the fire to brood.

A good part of him suspected that alchemy was so much nonsense, conceived and perpetuated by rascals and mountebanks to bilk the credulous of their savings. And yet he knew there were substances—opium, for one, lye for another, and gunpowder for a third—that were highly reactive under the proper circumstances. Gunpowder, for example, was a mixture of ingredients that, when exposed to a spark or flame, produced most dramatic results. Perhaps heat was the missing component to his experiments. But then lye required none to do its work.

If only he could get his hands on the *Turba Philosophorum*, one of the ancient texts on the subject. That wasn't bloody likely in the New World. He sighed and wished he'd thought of it before leaving London. Such a text would be devilishly hard to come by now, even if the locals weren't trying to kill him.

Much as he loathed the idea, he needed to make friends in town. Margaret had gone in today, but he would have to go in himself tomorrow. "Friends" would have resources of their own, access to things, to knowledge, he lacked.

Sometime after midday, he heard the opium whispering to him, promising dark, wonderful things. Desperate for distraction, he picked up his translation of the writings of Mithridates VI, king of ancient Pontus, who studied poison and poisonings extensively. For a while, Will was engrossed, inspired even, but eventually the drug's siren call became too powerful. He wanted more, felt he deserved it, told himself it would be his decision and not the opium's. All the same, he craved *the fat weed, that roots itself on Lethe wharf.*

And he feared it, too. And the more he thought about it, the more he feared it.

In an instant, he determined to bury the stuff—not destroy, but bury: its dark magic was too valuable to be cast aside forever—but he would certainly place it beyond convenience's reach.

He battled to his feet, rushed to the shelf where he'd stashed it and cast about for something sturdier in which to store it. It was already wrapped as it had been, but he wound it further in a bit of oilcloth and then placed it inside a small earthenware pot with a lid. This, too, he wrapped in oilcloth before carrying the whole package outside. He then fetched a spade from the plentiful store of tools the Jamieson family had left behind and set about finding the perfect spot to bury his burden. He thought it best to stash it as far from his cottage as possible, whilst still leaving it on his property, *as* his property. He hoped never to sample it again, but believed, too, that he wasn't quite done with it, either. After some minutes' search, he found a large stone, almost too big to budge, and wrestled it aside, that he might dig his hole. It was not a wide hole, once finished, but it was as deep as the spade's reach would allow. With no little relief, Will tossed his package into its depths and began replacing the dirt. By the time he was finished, he was drenched through with sweat and his arms, legs and back were complaining in a dozen places. But he'd succeeded in his mission; he'd made the opium devilishly hard to retrieve, decreasing, by some great measure, the likelihood that he'd ever access it again out of mere boredom or curiosity.

Returning to the cottage, he cleaned himself up with a damp cloth, changed his clothes (ever thankful that he was wealthy enough to do so) and laid down for a brief nap.

"Oh, what a shameless slugabed!" Margaret's voice rang out, "While the lady of the house is off braving the dangers of wilderness and rustic society, the master wallows in indolence!"

Will rolled onto his side and heaved himself into a sitting position. "Hardly," said he. "I've been doing some rather strenuous gardening, as a matter of fact."

"Have you?" Margaret's eyebrows shot up in mock surprise. "And what did you plant?"

"Opium," Will replied, rubbing some life back into his face.

"Opium? Do you mean to cultivate it?"

Now, it was Will's turn to look surprised. "I hadn't thought of that. I'll wager the folks hereabout would pay almost any price once they acquired the taste for it. But no. The stuff's too dangerous for that."

"What, then?"

"I buried it beyond temptation. Nothing short of Armageddon will convince me to fetch it forth."

"Then why not destroy it altogether?"

"Because I haven't ruled out Armageddon."

Margaret offered her hand, and Will used it to pull himself to his feet, grunting and groaning under his breath.

"Injuries still hurting?" Margaret asked.

"Everything is hurting. *When sorrows come, they come not single spies, but in battalions.*"

"I rather thought that was meant for greater woes than bad knees and a worse temperament."

"It is that," Will chuckled. "But growing old's a bawd."

"Surely, it beats the alternative."

"How did you fare in the village?"

"How but well? I was not devoured by goblins in the forest, not assailed by villains, not even insulted by self-righteous gossips. I was able to purchase everything on our list, and I even inquired about a dog, should one become available. Oh, and I almost forgot," she added, "I bought you a couple of new pipes." These she handed over to her clearly delighted friend. And yet, it wasn't long before his smile faded.

"Any news of Xander?" he said.

Margaret grew somber, too. "None."

Will feared as much, but rather than dwell on the obvious conclusion, pursued a different subject. "No sign of the men who attacked you?"

"I did not say that," Margaret allowed. "Just that they hadn't the nerve to confront me. I only saw two of them, anyway. The third and fourth were missing."

"I suppose it's too much to hope I limed one o' them."

"Do you know," said Margaret, "that I haven't even surveyed the scene?"

"Nor I," Will answered. "How could I be so stupid?"

"In fairness, you were suffering from multiple injuries."

"Nonetheless, the culprits may have left evidence of their identities behind. Perhaps even a body!"

Margaret laughed at this but agreed to accompany her friend to the back side of their home, to investigate the scene of the ambush. The back facing east, there was more than enough sunlight to reveal the tiniest of clues, but even a blind man would have noticed the enormous tracks wandering all over the yard, through dirt and grass alike.

"It's our monster," Will said, suddenly finding it difficult to breathe. "Has he been trying to get inside, I wonder?"

"What makes you think it's *male*?"

Will paused at this. "Excellent point. It would be foolish to assume anything. And, as we've said, it may not even be the only one of its kind in this wilderness."

"They didn't mention this in the advertisements…" Margaret cracked, desperate to lighten the tone.

"There is something…missing, here."

"How do you mean?"

Will rubbed his scalp, scratched at a dry patch. "A creature like this would be worth a fortune back in London, alive or dead, in private collections, zoos, the bear-baiting pits. There be hunters have killed or captured the largest, most fearsome of beasts—tigers, elephants, crocodiles. If our monster had been this frequent a visitor these past ten years or so, he'd have been caught by now, no?"

Following the thread of his thoughts, Margaret said, "Which

suggests it is a recent immigrant to these parts."

"The question is why? It can't be drawn to human flesh; the natives have been here forever."

"Perhaps," Margaret ventured, "it prefers the taste of Englishmen?"

Will laughed, dark as the notion was. "Not without mustard!" He then proceeded to follow the creature's meanderings about the yard. "There's none of my blood here, nor of the man I shot."

"You think our monster lapped it up like a dog?"

"It looks that way."

"Here's a handprint!" Margaret gasped. "I think."

Will hobbled to her side and squinted into the dirt. Indeed, there was a rather hand-like print, albeit two or three times the size of a normal hand. Then, too, this one seemed to have claws or lengthy nails.

"That's no bear," Margaret confirmed.

"No. Nor no man, neither."

"What, then?"

Will continued to stare at the print. "Caliban."

"Or Sycorax." After a brief silence, Margaret asked, "Should I go back inside and get your musket and pistol?"

"Call me a fool, but I don't believe our monster's in love with the sun. If it does return, it won't be before nightfall. Let's go scout the area my attackers were hid."

Again, they saw evidence the monster had thoroughly inspected the place, but no sign of bloodshed, of arrows, or anything else of note, though it did look as if something or someone had been dragged off into the woods.

"The ones I didn't hit pulled the injured fellow off this way," said Will.

"Was he dead, though, or merely wounded?"

"Shouldn't be hard to find out. I need to go into town tomorrow, anyway."

"But I've just gone," Margaret complained.

"Yes," Will agreed, "but I, too, have to make an appearance, that our enemies will know they have not cowed us."

"And hopefully," said Margaret, "I will get more accomplished in your absence than you did in mine."

~ 17 ~

Let Every Man Be Master of His Time

Jamestown, June, 1619

He got about halfway to town when he realized he'd no idea what day it was. Maybe church was in session, and he'd be expected to participate. It would be difficult to avoid if everyone else in the village was going. And there would be no one with whom he could chat if he managed to escape the pews, defeating the point of his going thither in the first place. But perhaps it wasn't Sunday. He'd done some gambling in his time and decided the odds were in his favor.

How had he forgotten what day it was, though? And was it July already, or still June? This business of having no business was surely disorienting. For years, he'd had a semi-regular routine and countless friends and associates to rouse him when he failed to make an appointment or meet a deadline. He'd come to find that lifestyle wearying.

But so, in its own way, was indolence.

If he'd been capable of building the palisade around his new home, he'd have kept himself occupied for some time, and perhaps even worked off some of the fat that had settled 'round his midriff. He was old, yes, but not antique. Her Majesty had lived to almost seventy, and she'd been nearly sedentary that last decade or so. If Will could remain active in mind and body and improve his diet, he might yet outlive the old harridan.

Always assuming he wasn't murdered by the locals or eaten by Caliban first.

Will thought again about the possibility their monster

was female, might even have offspring...and something, some wisp of an idea, fragment of memory tickled his brain, teased him, but would not fully reveal itself, something about female monsters and their get...

Gods, his feet ached. Especially the base of his great toes, where they joined his feet. They felt as if they'd been shattered with a blacksmith's hammer, an experience Will had mercifully never endured, but could well imagine nonetheless. But it was always thus, of late. He'd start out on a walk in reasonable comfort and, after a certain but never consistent distance, the pain would start. He could play the stoic with the best of 'em, but he was no glutton for punishment, either. He would make it to town and hire himself a ride back when the time came. What was wealth for, if not to purchase relief from unnecessary suffering?

Still, the pain distracted him from other, darker worries. Even with his pistol in hand, he did not think he could survive another ambush by the villains who'd assaulted him before. And, as ever, the monster lurked, in his mind, if not in his vicinity. A dignified gentleman did not run, but Will would have done so, had his feet allowed it.

In time—an eternity, by some measures—he got to Jamestown and discovered it was not in fact Sunday. Or, if it was, the population had forsaken its faith in favor of business, chores, and neighborly gossip. He looked anyone who happened to glance his way directly in the eyes, the better to gauge their reactions to his continued existence or, at a minimum, their attitudes about him in general. No one avoided his gaze, but neither did anyone hold it for long. He took that as a hopeful sign. He had his enemies, clearly, but the bulk of Virginians, it seemed, were indifferent to him and his presence, at worst. And least that was so on this day.

Per his previous visits, there was a small gathering of folks in front of the church and another by the storage building-cum-market. Will chose the market crowd, where, again, he happened upon the colony's governor.

"You're limping, Master Kemp," the man said.

Will nodded. "I'm afraid my feet have mounted an insurrection 'gainst my body."

The governor smiled at this. "You are a poet, sir. But how will you discipline these rebels, being, as they are, organs of the very body politic?"

"Marry, sir, if they cannot toe the line or come to heel, I'll have 'em whipped!"

"Would that not pain you all the more?"

"Truly, sir, but 'twould be a pain of mine own choosing, and oftentimes such burdens seem lighter than those imposed upon us by ungrateful tyrants."

Sir George raised an eyebrow at this. "Tyrants, sir?"

"It boots me not to flatter 'em, 'i faith, and yet must I tread softly, lest their petulance leave me powerless."

"Well," said the other man, "I am sorry to hear of your discomfort. Life is difficult enough without such annoyances."

"That it is, sir. Which is why I've come to tell you I have been attacked by someone here in town, as has my lady-friend."

The governor did not seem surprised by this. "I had heard rumblings."

"Had you? And who shall bring these ruffians to justice?"

"I'll do't, Master Kemp. You may depend upon it. But were you injured in this attack?"

"I took an arrow in the shoulder and another in my arm, here," Will said, stripping his sleeve enough to expose the damage.

"Arrows?"

"It cannot be the Powhatans," Will protested preemptively. "Surely they're more proficient with their bows."

Sir George nodded, wordlessly, as if Will's comment made all the sense in the world.

"And," Will continued, "I shot one of 'em."

"Did you?"

"I'm certain of it. I heard his cry of pain, along with a great deal of grunting from his fellows as they dragged him off into the woods. Has anyone gone missing here in town? Anyone come down with an unexplained injury?"

"I shall investigate, you have my word upon it. But, look you, on another matter, some of us are putting together a council of sorts, a House of Burgesses, if you will, to satisfy the other colonists, but also to aid me in governing our growing population. Would you consider joining us?"

"Me?" Will was astonished. "Why me?"

"Come now, sir. It's no secret you've the largest collection of books this side of the Atlantic. You seem a man of education, and I know you're a man of means. A gentleman, even. Why pretend otherwise?"

"Cannot a fellow be a new man in the New World? Or must he be forever shackled to Old World habits?"

"I ask only that you consider it. Ponder it a while before accepting or declining."

Will squinted into the distance, wondering how to proceed. He would never accept, he knew, but he could not afford to alienate the governor, the most powerful potential ally a man could have in Virginia. Rather than answer, he said, "Perhaps you've heard my apprentice has gone missing."

"I have." The man had ears everywhere. "But I know nothing of the specifics."

"We were visited by some of the natives. They marveled at the boy and expressed a strong desire to take him with them when they left. I thought I had placated them, but it seems they reappeared and took him anyway."

"And naturally you've searched for him."

"Of course," said Will. My companion and I spent an entire day looking for him."

"You're convinced the Powhatans have taken him?"

"My friend saw them. That is but one possibility, however."

"You see others?"

"He may have fallen prey to the same villains that assaulted my lady friend and me. Or he may have been…taken…by this beast that roams this wilderness."

"Or," said the governor, "he may have wandered off, as boys are wont to do, and simply gotten lost."

"No, sir," Will insisted. "Not this boy. He is far too bright for such foolishness."

"I will organize a party to search again, and I will speak to the local werowance, find out if he knows anything."

"It likes me well. But, again, there is this…monster…in the

forests hereabouts. What's being done about it?"

The governor removed his hat and wiped his brow with his left arm, visibly dampening his shirt sleeve. "This," he signed, "is why we need our House of Burgesses. Too many problems, all at once. More than any one man can cope withal. To answer your question, however, we have been hunting it constantly. It has, as you might imagine, a somewhat better understanding of the surrounding land than most of us and has proven rather elusive."

"It—or one of its brethren—has visited my lands on at least two occasions since I arrived." Will remarked.

This was, finally, was news to Sir George. "Has it? I wonder..."

Will cut him off. "We're isolated, aren't we? By choice, of course, but nonetheless we're easier, more vulnerable targets."

"Would you consider moving back into town until this beast has been found and killed?"

Will frowned. "That would mean moving farther away from Xander, if he still lives."

A lengthy silence grew between the two men, and, just as Will was about to make his farewells, the governor said, "There is one other thing..."

Will waited, his face open, patient.

"The locals miss you in church o' Sunday. That could be a problem for you, in time."

"The Almighty," Will responded, "being omniscient, knows me well. Better than I know myself, I daresay. I would not presume to suppose my presence in a particular building will either please or displease Him, but trust that He will let me know."

"And if this string of misfortunes you've endured of late are evidence of His dissatisfaction?"

"I hardly think our Lord so petty as to spirit away an innocent boy to punish me."

It was obvious the governor had more to say, but bit his lip and offered nothing further, which, from Will's perspective, spoke well of the man's judgement and self-discipline.

Will doffed his hat and swept it before himself in a great,

flamboyant arc. "I thank you for your time," said he, "and trust we'll speak again, anon."

It was the longest conversation he'd had with anyone outside of Margaret or Xander in weeks, and he revisited parts of it in his mind and aloud over and over for the next several minutes. He noted but little cared about the stares of passersby as he chatted away with himself, tasting the quality of each word or phrase he or the governor had uttered. There were things he might have said with greater elegance and eloquence, but "more matter and less art" echoed in his brain. If he could not be Portia, he would not be Polonius, either.

He was aware the locals' moods were malleable, easily shaped when gold was on offer. And so, they were friendly to his face, only too eager to please when he was looking to purchase anything. He thought of Timon, then, and promised himself he'd never fall so low. He would give and spend when he list and only to improve his own situation.

There was a man in town to whom everyone went with their injuries and ailments, who knew "a little medicine," and sometimes worked with a local midwife who assisted him in treating more serious cases. His name was Wotton, and hers, Mrs. Hobbs. They were as unlikely a pair as fire and ice— he, being warm and jovial, and she, cold and aloof. Between them, they determined that Will's wounds did not smell of sickness, were not unduly warm to the touch, and were not life-threatening. Yet. They wanted to cauterize the wound in Will's shoulder and stitch up that in his left forearm. Neither proposal pleased him, but at least they hadn't recommended leeches. He hated the damnable things beyond his ability to articulate. Wotton, it turned out, was one of Jamestown's earliest settlers, and distracted Will with tales of the Starving Time, whilst Mrs. Hobbs placed a red-hot surgical tool into his shoulder. Will thought he might scream, but, as the burning began, discovered the pain was not nearly as bad as he'd been expecting. He lost the thread of Wotton's narrative for a moment pondering this development. Perhaps, as someone who lived with some degree of pain every day of his life, he'd become inured to it. Or maybe it was just that the magnitude of this particular pain was not great enough to be truly bothersome.

Once he was sufficiently seared and sutured, Will asked whether Wotton or Mrs. Hobbs had any medicines they'd be willing to sell him, living, as he did, on the very edge of the wilderness. Wotton happily obliged him with tincture-of-this and extract-of-that and a salve or two of dubious composition. Whether they worked as intended was all one to Will; he was more interested in their alchemical properties. He might even be able to use them to make poison, something he could not purchase outright without raising questions amongst his fellow citizens.

Will thanked Wotton and Mrs. Hobbs for their care and offered them coin, which they gladly accepted. He made a mental note to revisit Wotton for more tales of early Jamestown, for, as far as Will was concerned, information was even more valuable than medicine.

At last, he had all the goods he could carry and all the information he was like to receive. It was time to hire a ride back home.

~ 18 ~

A HIT, A VERY PALPABLE HIT!

Jamestown, June, 1619

The sun was high and hot by the time the old man and his wagon delivered Will to the edge of his property, and his clothing was again soaked through with sweat. There were days like this in England, but Virginia promised an entire season of the same. The cottage's small root cellar seemed the only refuge from the heat, what though it felt more like a grave. Will remained in no rush to fill one.

Always, his feet stiffened up after a rest, following a lengthy walk, so that the brief hobble from the old man's wagon to his own front door was the most painful part of the day's journey. He forgot about his discomfort, however, when he passed through the palisade around his home and found himself in a sea of small stones, ranging in size from that of eggs all the way up to the hens who laid them. Upon further inspection, he saw the front and sides of his home had been battered by these same, with the shudders over his windows taking the most damage. For an instant, it was difficult to breathe. Then, he realized the door was still shut. Most likely, Margaret was safe behind it. Most likely. He could well imagine other possibilities, whose shades forced caution from him when every instinct demanded he rush the door.

Taking a deep breath, he drew his flintlock, checked that it was still ready to fire, and approached. "Margaret?" he said aloud.

"Will?" came the muffled reply.

"It is I," he called back.

There was much rattling and rustling on the door's opposite side as Margaret unbarred and cracked it just wide enough to confirm Will's identity. That done, she pulled it all the way open. "Thank God you've returned!"

"I tire of these jackanapeses, these whoreson ruffians," Will growled in exasperation.

Margaret led him inside the cottage, aware of the pain in his feet, even if he said nothing of it. "You think it the same men and not the natives?"

"There's one way to find out: we'll ask our neighbor if his or any other Virginian's home has ever been thus abused. If it's not some strange Powhatan practice, I'll wager it's our *friends* from town. But," said Will, "I needs must rest first. These feet of mine, these traitorous, insurrectionist feet, will humor me no farther for the nonce."

Margaret laughed. "Such drama! And you've sweated through your doublet."

"Aye, well, it's hot today," Will responded, throwing himself down in his chair. "As hot as...I know not what."

"You savor more and more of Falstaff every day."

"The man's wisdom is underappreciated, 'tis certain. A cup of wine!"

Again, Margaret laughed, fetching her friend his drink. "I'd have thought Harry a better model, or great Prosper."

"Fie!" Will spat. "A man wants pleasure in his age, but garners only ague, aches and incontinence."

"I hope not!" Margaret teased, "Remembering we share a bed."

But Will had no retort. It was his custom of an afternoon to nap, and he'd already gone to it with gusto, leaving his wine untouched and his clothing unchanged.

Good Sir John would never allow even a dram of wine to go to waste, though, and neither did Will. Upon awakening from his slumber, he spied the still-untouched cup on the table nearby and bolted it. No harm in paying homage to Dionysus, after all. And Will knew he would ache, as he always did coming out of a nap after a long walk. The wine would help.

"Old do I wax, and from my weary limbs, honor is cudgeled," he groused as he struggled to rise.

From the other room, Margaret exploded with merriment. "Honor?" said she. "If sleeping be honorable, you're a saint by now!"

"Hush woman!" Will insisted. "I am allowed some poetic license." Margaret came into the room, in case he needed her assistance, but he did not, or stubbornly would not admit to it. "I'm going outside for a bit. I need to piss, and then I'll consider these stones about our home."

"Shall I come with you?"

"For the pissing, or the stones?

"Why, the stones, of course."

"Why the stones, indeed."

"To frighten us away, I imagine." Margaret said, not willing to encourage his wordplay further.

They ventured out into the afternoon sunshine, Will growing more limber with each step. He held up a hand, so she knew not to follow him, and wandered off beyond the palisade. Meantime, she studied the cottage's walls, assessing the damage.

"It's not just these stones," Will raged upon his return. "They've torn up our vegetables and killed all my pretty chickens!"

Bewilderment flashed across Margaret's face, and her mouth hung open as she gathered her thoughts. "Do they think to starve us out?"

Will nodded. "Or, by an onslaught of general hostilities, drive us away and back to England. Still, the chickens, too? What dogs are these?" He pulled on his beard in the ensuing silence, staring at the stones around the yard. "What did you hear?" he asked his companion.

"Hear? Nothing," Margaret answered.

"During the bombardment. Did the blows against the side of our house assume a pattern? Did they come in twos or threes or fours? Or were there indeed so many that no pattern was evident?"

Margaret thought back to that attack. "Twos, I think, and for a good while."

"Two men," said Will. "As I thought. You said three or four assaulted you, and we know I hit at least one with my pistol when I was ambushed. Two would explain why they didn't attempt to break in and harm you further—they weren't certain they would succeed. And bullies, you know, are often cowards." With that, he began gathering the stones and tossing them into a pile.

Margaret quickly followed his example. Until one caught her eye. "Ha!" she exclaimed. "This one's got the print of a finger on it, a thumb, if I'm not mistaken."

"Does it?" Will turned towards her immediately. "Let me see."

Margaret passed him the stone in question, which he then stared at for some time before speaking.

To her surprise, he brought it to his nose and sniffed. "*This pitch, as ancient writers do report, doth defile...*" He murmured to himself. "I believe we can use this to identify one of our suspects."

"Yes?"

"A plan begins to present itself," Will said, squinting towards the sun. "Let us see if there are other such prints, gather those stones, and take them inside. I have some drawing to do."

"But perhaps you can, er, freshen up a bit first?" Margaret said, not ungently. "Have a little rinse in the stream while the day's still warm?"

Will grabbed the neck of his shirt, pulled it away from his body and took a goodly whiff. "Gods!" he japed. "*Give me an ounce of civet, good apothecary, to sweeten my imagination!*"

A brief wash and fresh set of clothing later, Will sat again at his table, with paper, quill and ink at the ready. In one hand he held the stone, in the other, a sort of lens through which he examined it. Margaret had opened the shutters to help in this endeavor and also placed a candle nearby.

"Making notes, then?"

"I'm going to reproduce this print on a much larger scale," Will answered. "If I can. When we see this print again, we'll have our man."

"And how do you plan to obtain another such print?"

"The play's the thing!" Will cackled, deviously.

~ 19 ~

FOR ORPHEUS' LUTE WAS STRUNG WITH POETS' SINEWS

Jamestown, July, 1619

"Why did you never write in Latin, like some of your fellows?" Margaret asked Will after dinner.

"Writing in Latin is like gifting a jewel-encrusted scabbard to a friend who owns no sword."

That answer having satisfied Margaret, she then said, "And will you truly write no more?"

"No more blank verse, at any rate. It's too familiar to me now, like an old hussif that will not be placated but by death."

"What then?"

Will was silent a while before answering. "Have you read this tale of Cervantes'? The Spaniard?"

"I've heard bits and pieces, only," Margaret replied.

Will struggled to find words to explain his impressions of the work. "It is like an epic poem without the verse, a bedtime story made elegant. And it requires no vainglorious actors, no props, no costumes, no scripts. You may piece out its imperfections with your thoughts, as it were. And all of the profit—all of it— goes to the author."

"I wasn't aware you wrote for profit."

"There's little I haven't done in pursuit of a shilling. Why should writing be any different?"

Margaret nodded, as if to say, "Who am I to judge?" What she *did* say was, "Then you will be writing a tale of your own?"

"And why not? Do not these meadows, these trees, these

hills inspire you? Am I less out of my humor than Alonso Quixano? Any less mad than Don Quixote?"

"His giant was a windmill, as I have heard. Yours is an actual monster, one that tears men into pieces before devouring them. And...I make a poor Dulcinea."

"Perhaps you are my Sancho, then."

Margaret scowled. "I'll take Dulcinea. I can grow into the role."

Will smiled. "I never doubted you."

"Your bread improves," Will said over another meal.

"It could hardly have been worse," Margaret replied, dunking a bite-sized fragment into her wine before popping it into her mouth. "When will the palisade be finished?"

"What day is this? I forgot to ask in town."

"Saturday."

"Then the crew resumes work the day after tomorrow, on Monday, at which point we shall have the answers to many of our questions."

"Do you think our nemeses killed Xander?"

Will put down his own wine, swallowed, and said, "The possibility has crossed my mind." It was not a confession that came easily. He'd made a promise to Lucy, and if the lad was indeed his own, the failure to protect him was damning.

"And if we determine that they did, will the boy ever have justice?"

Eager to move on, Will said, "If we can prove they killed him, yes, I trust the governor to see justice done. The proving, however, will be the difficult thing. But I am not yet ready to concede his death. I cannot. Come Monday, as I said, we shall know more."

Now, the master of the house had, amongst his cabinet of curiosities, a lute—a forlorn, neglected thing that had oft drawn Margaret's eye. She picked it up and turned to its owner. "May I?"

"If you can coax anything more than dissonance from that," Will smirked, "you're a better man...a better *person* than I."

Margaret ignored his misstep and began plucking the strings and adjusting the pegs. Will leaned back in his chair, impressed. "Is there nothing you cannot do?"

"I cannot be Queen," she said matter-of-factly and started to play.

Will closed his eyes appreciatively and nodded in time to the music. Anon, he said, "It's a melancholy melody, that."

"Would you rather a merry?"

"No, no," said he. "It likes me well and suits the time as feathers do a bird." The food of love, indeed.

Margaret smiled, but remained quiet, allowing the lute to speak on her behalf. Without segue, she launched into *Barbry Allen.*

"And a lovely voice you have, too. Of course!" Will observed.

The sun went down, his sister rose, and neither Will nor Margaret could have said how much time they passed in her music. When at last she placed the lute back on its shelf, Will said, "Oh, how I envy your talent!"

"Nonsense!" she answered. "Your quill is your lute and hath no equal in this world."

It was a sweet thing to say. Will reached across the table and took Margaret's hand in his. He would have held it still, but she rose sometime later to go to bed.

"'Tis time," she said. "And past time. And if you sleep in that chair again, you'll curse yourself come morning."

"There's nothing new in that."

~ 20 ~

THE CLIMATE'S DELICATE,
THE AIR MOST SWEET

Jamestown, July, 1619

The world was a bewildering cacophony of knocking and pounding, come Monday. Margaret groaned and sat up beside him.

"It must be mid-morning already," she observed.

"Too much wine?" Will asked.

"Yes, but what's your excuse, you slugabed?"

It was true, too. He enjoyed his bed entirely too much these days. He could have done without the noise, though. "I expect that's the crew at work on the palisade," said he.

"And someone's at the door, as well," Margaret added.

Will swung his legs off the bed and slowly unfolded, unkinked, uncramped himself 'til he stood more or less erect. "Suppose I'd better get it, then." He shuffled into the front room. "Yes, yes! I'm coming."

The knocking ceased, but the pounding, the hammering, continued.

Reaching the door at last, Will unbarred it and cracked it open a handspan to see what the matter was. The Lord Governor stood on his front step with two other men at his back.

"Late night, Master Kemp?" he inquired.

"That it was," Will said. "What can I do for you, Sir George?"

"For me? No, no. I'm here for you and yours. I've got that scouting party I promised just behind your wall here—impressive, by the way, and not a bad idea in these times—and I came by to ask if you'd be interested in joining us?"

A thousand worries crossed Will's mind in the moment: the fear of leaving Margaret alone with the workers, that fear of getting too far into the forest and falling prey to the monster or the Powhatans, and, finally, the knowledge that another long walk would leave him hobbled for days. And yet, he did not want to appear ungrateful or cowardly. But as it seemed the governor was his only ally at the moment, he could not decline. "Certainly!" he declared. "Give me a moment to gather my things, and I shall be delighted to accompany you."

Margaret was less than pleased with the idea, knowing he'd be of little use for the remainder of the day and perhaps the next two or three. Still, she helped him dress, filled his waterskins, and even loaded his musket. The pistol, he insisted she keep, as neither of them trusted the crew building the palisade. Will fetched his sword and packed a few things to eat, and stepped outside. His worries diminished considerably the instant he heard the bar fall into place behind the door. If any of these workers meant harm to Margaret, they'd have to work like the dickens to get at her, at the probable cost of their own lives.

Soon, he stood in the yard between his cottage and the palisade, pipe in one hand and a cane in the other. The day was overcast, with a fair breeze out of the southeast. It would be, to Will's profound relief, a day without too much sweating.

"You made good time!" the governor said as Will approached.

"I hate to be kept waiting," Will replied. "I can only assume that's true for others, as well."

"A sound conclusion," said Sir George, slapping Will on the back near his injury and gesturing the way forward with his other hand.

Wincing, Will cast a final glance at the men building his wall and, seeing nothing sinister in their bearing, dismissed his worries for the time being.

"You have no horse, sir?" he asked Sir George upon spying the search party.

"On the contrary," the governor said, "I have a magnificent beast. But you have not, and a searching party can only travel at the speed of its slowest member."

"Marry, sir, I know not which is worse, that you do think me slow or, worse, a 'member.'" Will would play with words 'til the pox took him, 'til he sailed across the river Styx. It was more than a habit, by now. It was an addiction. Even with no one 'round to hear him, he punned and rhymed and turned meanings inside out.

"You have a way with words, sirrah, that makes a man to wonder," Sir George offered, diplomatically.

"I'd rather a way with women, but at my age, I'll take whate'er is offered."

The rest of the party chuckled good-naturedly and turned for the forest.

The walk gave Will plenty of time to learn about the governor, the Jamestown colony, and Virginia in general. The natives— 'savages,' as Sir George and the rest of the party deemed them— were indeed as changeable as Will had been led to believe. Still, the men held them in less suspicion, less contempt than the Spanish, who were thought to have agents everywhere, even, perhaps, amongst their own number. This gave Will pause. Could a Spaniard ape English so well as to conceal his own accent? He studied the other men as they moved along through the wilderness and felt the cold finger of paranoia creep up his belly and lodge in his bosom. To divert himself from his growing unease, he asked the names of the various plants, birds and insects they encountered along the way. The governor and his fellows were able to answer many of his questions with terms the settlers had given things, or with Powhatan names, but a stubborn portion remained unknown and unnamed to everyone. As a lover of words, Will was torn: on the one hand, things without names were cyphers, on the other, they again justified his coming hither, to encounter and experience the unfamiliar, the new.

The bald cypress was a case in point. There were no trees like it in England, Wales, Scotland or Ireland, and none in mainland Europe, either. These majestic and often defiant trees seemed utterly magical. And there were various pines, as well, whose size and aromatic qualities, Will was certain, would have made any timber trader pant with greed, for they had never known the axe and would provide timber of unparalleled quality. Men being what they were, he feared there would be none of them left in a few generations.

The party stopped to rest and refresh itself after a couple of hours, at which point, one of the men asked Will about his goals in the New World, about what he'd left behind and hoped to discover in Virginia. Will shared as much of his plans and history as he deemed possible without self-incrimination, then deftly redirected the conversation away from himself.

"This monster that haunts these woods," said he, "is my greatest fear in this new land. Has anyone seen it?"

"I've heard rumors of sightings of course," Sir George confessed. "But rumors only."

Disliking that answer, Will protested, "I have seen plenty of tracks. You've seen plenty of remains. We know the beast is large, voracious, and without mercy. How has it managed to escape capture or death?"

"It's not about in daylight, is it?" a pockmarked fellow named Salt replied. "And none of us are fool enough to go a-hunting in the dark with anything less than an army."

"Yes, yes," Will said. "So Sir George informs me. But what about traps? Poison? Surely, there must be expert hunters amongst the other settlers."

"For hunting bears, wolves and such, we've plenty of capable men. But this is no working-day beastie."

"If we all hunted it down, the lot of us? Surely, there's safety in numbers," Will said.

"Or we'd be making it easier for the damned thing to kill more of us."

"And no one in town's been attacked. Why take such a drastic measure unless the actual townsfolk are in jeopardy."

"Then the outliers, like the Jamiesons, like me, we're to fend for ourselves?"

"I'm here helping you look for your boy, am I not?" Salt replied with an edge to his voice. "But for charging off into the night so some monster can gut me? No, thank you."

"You chose to purchase the Jamieson place," another man

pointed out. "You might have built in town."

"Now, now," said Sir George, "there's naught to be gained from this kind of talk. We are all Virginians now and must do what we can for one another."

His words seemed to mollify the others, but Will saw the lay of the land—if the combined weight of all his other misadventures since arriving had not communicated it already: he was an outsider, and his needs would be the last priority in town if and when hardship befell them all.

Hours into the search, Will was spent and dreaded the thought of the long trek back home. The presence of the others had given him the confidence, the comfort, to truly observe his surroundings without fear of attack, but though this buoyed his spirits for a time, he was ready to admit defeat and crawl back into his cottage. He'd had enough of walking and conversation to last the rest of the month and then some. They would not find Xander today. And he was not entirely disappointed when Sir George called a halt to their search, in the interest of getting back to town before dark.

"Gentlemen," he said, "I am most grateful for your efforts on my behalf."

The group acknowledged his comment with nods and grunts only; none offered words of encouragement, and it seemed understood that the boy was either dead or had taken up with the natives, never to be seen again.

On the long, physically agonizing trip home, Will punished himself—as only a man of his talents could do—with every sort of recrimination imaginable and more than a few of the unimaginable variety. Why hadn't he gotten to know the lad better? Why hadn't he protected him more? Why had he agreed to bring him hither in the first place? Was Will not the very paragon of perfidy? Not, after all, the most selfish fellow who'd ever lived? Whoreson rogue enough to put even Falstaff to shame?

Or was he not, instead, the most self-indulgent actor the world had ever seen?

Out on such self-pity! It was unmanly, unseemly and aloof

from the entire point: an innocent was living amongst the savages, lost or, most likely, dead. Will needed to learn the truth of it, that he might put the boy's spirt to rest…if necessary.

As they entered at last the Jamiesons' fields, Sir George said, "I cannot help but notice your gait has changed over these past few hours and deduce, thereby, that your insurrection has resumed. Gout, is it?"

"Ah," Will sighed ruefully, "you know the devil, do you?"

"My father suffered terribly from its bite, and so shall I in time, I suppose."

"I would not wish that fate on any man."

The governor nodded in agreement, and then added, "The Powhatans, though, have a sort of—what shall I call it?—broth? That they make from leaves or bark that doth wonders for the feet, the knees and other joints."

"And what do they call this miracle elixir?"

"There, I cannot help you. I can never remember their names for things," Sir George shrugged.

"Nonetheless," Will said, "I shall inquire after it."

"And will you join us in our House of Burgesses?"

Will paused for a moment, looked across his land, and stared at the lone oak near his cottage as if it might answer for him. When it had nothing to say on the matter, he said, "I humbly thank you for the opportunity, but I think I cannot. I've far too much work to do as it is, and governance has never been a strong suit of mine."

Sir George smiled. "You have already mastered the hardest part."

"And that is?"

"Saying no."

Will laughed. He could not help it. Of all the men he'd met in Jamestown, Sir George was by far the most amicable, the most pleasant. "You're always welcome to come by for a visit, whenever you need a reprieve from politics."

Now, it was Sir George who laughed. "I may just take you up on that, Master Kemp."

As they were just about to part, Will remembered a last issue he'd forgotten to raise with His Lordship. He looked past the governor to ensure the other men weren't listening, and then, in a low voice, asked, "Have you heard anything further of those ruffians who attacked us?"

The answer was in Sir George's face before it left his mouth. "I have not. But I shall continue to investigate."

Will was not as disappointed as he might have been, for a plan was beginning to take shape in his mind. He offered the governor and his fellows a hearty farewell and turned towards his cottage.

Margaret was only too happy to let him in, and he, beyond grateful to enter, for Margaret had been baking, and the place smelled of sweetcakes.

"You are a goddess," he exclaimed, "that you so easily summon the very perfume of culinary perfection."

She rolled her eyes at his flattery. "You must be hungry, or you'd not subject me to such hyperbole."

"Hyperbole?" Will gasped, laying a hand across his chest. "I am wounded."

"It's your flattery that's wounded."

"Well, it is but the first draft, the foul papers, if you will."

"Most foul, strange and unnatural."

"I grant you. It was a long, arduous walk, and I am past tired."

"And still no sign of Xander?" Margaret asked.

"No, nor of the natives, nor our monster, Caliban."

Margaret placed her hands on her hips, and, with an arched eyebrow, said, "What *did* you accomplish, then?"

"Oh," said Will, "I learned the names of many a bird, plant or insect. And a few of our fellow settlers. I learned fear of the Spanish still eclipses fear of our monster hereabouts."

"Truly? I think I'd rather be shot by a Spaniard than ripped asunder and eaten by a beast."

Per his custom, Will threw himself down in his chair by the fire. "And I," said he, "would rather you helped me remove these infernal boots."

"A fate easily as grisly as the other two," Margaret complained, though a mischievous twinkle possessed her eyes.

"You're fortunate you have only to smell my feet and not walk upon them, for I hold that hell can have no greater torment than old age."

"And yet, most would endure it over death."

"*Thus conscience does make cowards of us all…*"

The friends' banter continued in this fashion for some time, until, like clockwork, Will drifted into a doze. When he awoke, the last rays of sunlight were struggling through the shutters, and Margaret had placed a heaping bowl of pottage near his elbow. Will yawned, stretched and rubbed his face.

"Are we all locked up for the night, then?" he asked.

"Not quite," Margaret replied. "I've been a little busy making dinner. Do you think you can manage it?"

Will pushed himself to his feet, which somehow hurt less than they had the previous day, and walked to the door. The instant he dropped the bar into place across the door, it rattled and shook, causing Will to stumble backwards, startled. "Who's there?" he called. "What do you want?" He shot a look in Margaret's direction, but she was as confused as he.

The door rattled again, and again Will asked "Who is it? Who's there?" Immediately beyond the door, there was no answer, but farther out into the yard he thought he heard a voice. Then, a fist or other heavy object pounded on the door. Will took another step away from it. Without saying a word, he pantomimed firing a musket to Margaret, whereupon she nodded and fetched the weapon and a burning candle, with which to light the fuse. For herself, she then laid hands on the largest knife they owned.

Beyond the door, all sound had ceased.

"Well, it's not our monster," Will whispered. "Our Caliban, for I very much doubt he'd knock."

"Master Kemp?" a familiar voice called out.

Again, Will looked over to Margaret for confirmation that he wasn't imagining things. "Xander?" he asked her in disbelief.

"I think so."

"Xander?" Will repeated, much louder.

"Yes, sir. Would you let me in?"

Turning to Margaret, Will gestured to the door with the

barrel of his musket. She crossed to unbar it whilst he stood guard and, after an awkward few seconds, a face materialized in the candlelit gap between the door and jamb.

"Xander!" Margaret cried out.

But he was not alone. Off to either side of him stood native warriors, masked in the deepening shadows of evening.

"Come in, boy, come in!" Will urged. "You don't want to be out after dark."

"And my friends?"

Ah. His Powhatan escorts. For a moment, Will wrestled with the question, but ultimately decided if the worst came to pass and Caliban murdered the natives, the blame and the guilt would fall upon him. "Very well," he grumbled, "if needs must." He ushered the boy and his escort into the room and allowed Margaret to close and bar the door while he continued to scrutinize his visitors.

Immediately, Will threw his arms about the boy, hugging him close like a man on a sinking bark. If there were tears in his eyes as he did so, nobody noticed or commented. "I would ask where you've been," said he, "but I believe that's obvious. How and why, though, are very much in question. How comes it that you arrive just after I've returned from looking for you?"

"You were seen by family of the werowance. He sent me back, I reckon, as a gesture of good will."

The two natives standing by looked about for a moment before shuffling over to one wall and moving to sit at its base, facing the fire. The threat of violence or ambush seemingly having receded, Will leaned his musket against the table and studied Xander again. The boy—or his hosts—had shaved the right half of his head and painted the upper portion of his face a deep red.

"Well?" said Will.

"I..." Xander stuttered, "I felt...lost."

"E'en here?"

"Even here. And though I was ta'en against my will, I've been through worse."

Frustrated by this answer, Will asked, "Then why return?"

"I don't belong with the Powhatans, either. Oh, they'd

have me, but…" Xander trailed off, unable to put words to his thoughts.

It was Margaret, of course, who finally stepped forward to put an arm around the boy's shoulder and offer him welcome. "A good meal and some ale should put you right."

Xander smiled and exhaled, as if he'd been holding his breath, and, within minutes, all five of the cottage's occupants were enjoying a hearty repast. Will watched the natives as surreptitiously as possible, for he did not want to alarm them, though every minute in their presence spawned a thousand questions: Did they believe in God? Did they believe in an afterlife? What did they think of death? What were their women like and what was their role in Powhatan society? Had they seen any Spanish? How did they pass their days? What did they wear in winter? How did they get along with other groups of natives? How far had they explored to the south, west, and north? Did they have music?

What he asked was, "Do they have plays?"

Xander stared at him as if hedgehogs had just crawled from his nostrils. "Plays?"

"Yes, theatre, or anything like it."

"They have stories, legends."

Will's eyes lit up with boyish delight. "I should like to hear one."

Xander frowned. "I don't know their language well enough."

"No, no," said Margaret, "of course you wouldn't. It's only been—what?—a few weeks?"

"Can any of their folk speak English well enough?" Will wanted to know.

"The werowance, maybe."

"Really?" said Will. "The same werowance who pretends not to understand a word?" He glanced over at the natives, but neither was looking in his direction. "'Tis a wise man who knows more than he reveals. He bears watching. Still, I was hoping to learn of their experience with this monster."

"Wendigo," Xander offered.

"What? Wendigo? Is that its species or this individual creature's name?"

The boy shrugged. "That's what they call this one, I think." The two natives were now watching this exchange with evident interest and more than a little trepidation. Seeing this, Will turned to them. "Wendigo?"

One of the men flinched as if struck, the other covered his mouth with a hand and repeated the gesture, to be sure Will understood. Will assumed he was being told not to say the word, at least not in their current circumstance, trapped indoors, at night. He turned to Xander. "Have either of them ever seen it?"

Xander crossed the room and crouched next to the man who had gestured a moment earlier. He whispered a few words under his breath, but Will could make no sense of them. The native man responded and jabbed his companion in the shoulder with two fingers. This man, then, seemed to shrink into himself, while his eyes appeared to grow to thrice their size.

Xander looked back at Will and Margaret. "He says he has not, but Machk has. But it does not look as if Machk wants to speak of it."

Yet, there were other ways to communicate. Will rose and walked over to the shelf where he'd stashed paper, an inkwell and quill and retrieved them. He then joined his son and the natives on the floor, painful as the effort was on his knees. In a few strokes, he sketched out a rough image of a man. After glancing over to make certain the natives understood what he was asking, he offered the quill and paper to the man who'd allegedly seen the monster. He was reluctant to accept the challenge, until his friend urged him to it, whereupon he took the quill and, with great concentration, drew a much larger man next to the one Will had created. But then he added great, hooked claws, a bulge or hunch or the creature's back, monstrous teeth, and more. When he was finished, everyone leaned forward to get a better view of the image. After a few seconds, they all likewise pulled away as if frightened by the thing.

Will caught Xander's eye. "Is he saying it is that much larger than us?"

Xander said a single word, and both men replied with a single syllable. "Yes," said the boy. "It is that much larger than any of us."

"But that is one and a half times the height of a man..." Margaret breathed.

"And several times its weight, I don't doubt." Will stood, with some help from Xander. He must have had some strange expression on his face, for the others stared at him expectantly.

"What?" he asked.

"You looked as though you'd just thought of something," said Margaret.

Will ran a hand over his balding pate. "This thing is familiar to me, somehow."

It was a long night, what with the two Powhatans sleeping on the floor in the next room, and a galaxy of questions looming over everything. If Will slept at all, he was unaware of having done so. But, in his age—his *dotage*, he might have said—he'd become somewhat accustomed to sleepless nights and even learned to make use of them, imagining lines of verse, plots and characters for plays, and, sometimes, strategies for his financial advancement. This night, however, was mostly dedicated to the many dangers facing his little family.

The palisade was a good start, but a start only. Will continued to feel the need for artillery. And at least one dog. He hoped for a better relationship with his neighbors, too, that they might warn and protect one another as occasion demanded. But it seemed the locals were not as enamored of his friend Margaret as he, nor were they overjoyed with the presence of his son, Xander. That his new family was somehow distasteful to the people of Jamestown was, in turn, distasteful to him, for if there was one thing Will despised more than anything else, it was bigotry. He'd had enough of the animosity between Catholics and Protestants, for example, to last him a lifetime—another one—and the same could be said of the squabbles between the nobility and the merchant class. And then, nobody gave two figs for the poor. He'd been given to understand that when the first ships arrived in Jamestown, gentleman in the company refused to lift a finger in the way of manual labor, even to help in their own survival, but everything had been left to the commonfolk. As usual. He imagined that in Hell the wealthy did all the work whilst the poor stood by and enjoyed what little comforts they might.

If there was such a thing as Hell.

He'd enjoyed Marlowe's depiction of it, conventional as it was, largely because of the man's lyrical skill. But he was not convinced, for himself, that such a place or fate existed. The suffering and losses he'd seen and sometimes endured through disease, war and occasional poverty seemed every bit the equal of imagined lakes of fire and eternal torment. Could Hell be worse? And, if so, why? Had not he and most others he knew already made substantial down payments on the agonies of damnation? Did the Devil have a monopoly on the infliction of pain?

He did not. And, if not, whence came suffering? What was its point and purpose? Was it of God? Will had helped to create His Majesty's Bible. Had it not been written in John 3:16, "For God so loved the world that He gave His only begotten Son, that whosoever believeth in Him should not perish, but have everlasting life?" Was suffering the penalty then, for disbelief? How did that explain the suffering of those who *did* believe? And what sort of God threatens his creations into belief?

Kit had written, "I count religion but a childish toy and hold there is no sin but ignorance." How often Will reflected on that line he could not say, but felt that truer words were ne'er set down on parchment.

His weary brain wandered into thoughts of Xander, and then by natural progression to the boy's mother. "He is thine," she'd said as he'd lingered on the threshold between yes and no. Not 'yours,' but 'thine.' It was transparent, in retrospect. He'd been so needful of such news, she'd seen it before he had, and she'd hooked him with the seeming object of his most secret desires.

Why, look you now, how unworthy a thing you make of
me! You would play upon me; you would seem to know
my stops; you would pluck out the heart of my
mystery; you would sound me from my lowest note to
the top of my compass…

And he, ever the fool, had obliged her.

And yet, if it were true! A son! *His* son!

He had to do whatever was best for the boy, of course. The boy's needs were...what *did* he need? What were his aspirations?

Xander had changed since Will had seen him last. Had he grown? It seemed impossible in such a short time, and yet the boy was taller. Or Will had gotten shorter? Xander was calmer, too, more comfortable, it seemed, with his plight. Had he learned something from the natives that made it so? Whatever the case, Will resolved to take full advantage of this second chance at fathering the young man. He'd been too preoccupied before, but now he understood, again, that his salvation lay, not in Scripture, but in his son.

~ 21 ~

ONE TOUCH OF NATURE
MAKES THE WHOLE WORLD KIN

Jamestown, July, 1619

He was awakened by the sound of the door being opened. He could hear Xander saying something, but recognized not a syllable of it, and then the door closed again. As he did not hear the bar being replaced behind the door, he knew it was day before even opening his eyes. When he did, he saw that Margaret was already about her business and he, as usual, was the last out of bed. Not wishing to emulate the early gentlemen of Jamestown, he rolled into a sitting position with his legs dangling off the bed and gave his face a firm rubbing. It was an old actors' trick, but one that always made waking easier.

In the main room, he found Margaret cooking over the fire, whilst Xander puzzled over Will's book collection.

"Your friends have gone?" he inquired of his son.

"They have," Xander said offhandedly.

"Would you like to learn to read?" Will asked him.

"I can read. A little," the boy answered defensively.

"Of course. But better?"

Xander shrugged. "Why not?"

"Choose one, and let's have a look."

The boy shuffled through them for a moment before choosing a smaller, thinner volume. "What's this?"

Will laughed. "*Greene's Groatsworth of Wit.* As errant of piece of knavery, mark you now, as can be offered."

Xander made a face. "Doesn't sound interesting." He pulled another book. "And this one?"

"A favorite of mine!" Will beamed. "*The Prince*. It's all about political power—how to obtain it, how to maintain it..."

"No. And this?"

"That," said Will, "is about a great warrior who is summoned to fight a terrible monster. And later, he fights a dragon!"

"What's it called?"

"The dragon?"

"The book!"

"*Beowulf*."

"That's a funny title."

"It's the name of the hero," Will explained.

Carrying the book to the table, Xander sat and said, "Let's have this one, then."

Will glanced over at Margaret, seeking her permission or at least approval before he postponed his morning chores and started reading. The smile she offered him was permission enough.

"As you wish," he said, sitting down and pouring himself a cup of water before extending a hand to receive the book. A candle burned nearby, and he moved it closer as he opened the book and squinted at its text whilst his eyesight adjusted to this new challenge. Clearing his throat with a mighty harrumph, he began to read. Xander was bored at first, until Grendel made his first appearance in the tale, and then even Will sat up straighter and read with more vigor. In fact, he was so excited that he read through the passage a second time, as if to confirm some essential detail that he wasn't yet ready to share. This he did every time Grendel or his mother appeared in the story, only setting the book down once both monsters were dead.

"Is that it?" Xander asked.

"What?" Will asked, as if waking from a dream. "Oh. No, no. Beowulf still has to fight a dragon."

Xander's eyes lit up. "A dragon? Why did you stop?"

"Because," said Will, "I now believe Grendel and our Wendigo are one and the same. The same species, in any case."

"And how does that help us?" Margaret wondered aloud.

"It shows that our monster can be killed."

"But if Grendel was real," Margaret replied, "then isn't the dragon as well?"

Will pursed his lips in thought, scratched at a spot on the tabletop with a yellowed fingernail. At last, he blew out his lips and said, "We have some evidence of a Grendel. Let us worry about the fiend in front of us before we speculate on other monsters still to come."

Margaret placed a bowl of leftover stew and a piece of fire-warmed bread on the table in front of Will. "Sound advice."

"Can we hear about the dragon, now?" Xander inquired.

"You rascal!" Will chuckled accusingly. "I thought I was teaching you to read, not reading an entire book for your amusement!"

"Tut!" said Margaret. "A more willing victim I've never seen."

Everyone laughed at this, for it was undeniably true. Will loved to read, and, more than that, he loved to perform. Still, he would not surrender the notion he'd just stumbled upon, that Grendel and this Wendigo were relatives of a sort.

"Again, how does this help us?" Margaret demanded.

"Perhaps not at all," Will answered. "Or, perhaps it tells us that these creatures were hunted to extinction in Europe, which further shows they can be killed."

"That's small comfort," Margaret quipped.

Will leaned his head to one side, as if conceding the point. "Small is better than none."

Margaret sighed, dismissing the topic. "Eat your food, you boys. I'll not have it said the lady of the house serves cold food."

The boys ate, albeit with some little discussion of the day's chores that lay ahead of them, of the goals and hopes each held before the sun crept off behind the woods again.

The first order of business was to inspect the workers' progress on the palisade. This was little more than a convenient excuse, however, for as they walked the perimeter, Will asked the boy about his time away, where the Powhatans had taken him, how he'd been treated, and why they'd allowed him to return. Flora, fauna and monsters aside, the Powhatans remained the most fascinating of the New World's denizens. A part of Will was envious of his son's adventure.

According to the Xander, he'd gone outside one morning to practice throwing his dagger, when he'd spied a party of natives watching him from the tall grass. They had made no move to threaten or approach him, but, instead, had held up rabbits and fowl. Xander remained where he was, unmoved, until the Powhatans dropped their bows and other weapons, whereupon he moved some fifteen or twenty steps in their direction. When both sides had full view of the other, the natives sat, clearly making it easier for Xander to run away if he felt the need. Instead, as they'd intended, the boy felt emboldened and walked ever closer. One of the natives—the werowance, as Xander would come to learn—repeatedly patted the ground, which Xander took to be an invitation to join the natives. For a moment, he struggled with the idea, which he took to be a life-or-death decision.

And then he sat.

From a pouch at his waist, the werowance produced dried meat and offered it to Xander, which he accepted after some initial hesitation. If they meant to kill him, he reasoned, they could have done so already. Soon, without really knowing why, he wandered away with his new friends. Had he been bewitched? Xander didn't know or could not bring himself to care.

He travelled with the natives to the river, where they swam, drank and caught fish. It was, Xander confessed, the most he'd enjoyed himself since coming to Virginia. In time, the group resumed its journey, passing through one small village where the werowance received a number of gifts, before proceeding to another, slightly larger one, where they spent the rest of the day and ensuing night.

Naturally, Xander was the center of attention in both villages, for no one had ever seen a child with skin and hair like his. Some wanted bits of that hair, others wanted to view his entire anatomy, as if his fingers and toes, his ears, nose and privates might somehow be different than their own. They sniffed him, constantly, too, and laughed at his apparently unpleasant breath. This, they amended with certain grasses and leaves, which they forced him to chew until he was sick of the stuff. Some warriors there were who wanted Xander for their sisters or daughters—some, even, for their wives, or so he surmised. He was likewise gifted with tokens of their admiration in the form of special foods, of weapons, clothing, and jewelry, which made him marvel at the difference between the way he was treated back in England and then here, amongst the natives. Back home, he was an afterthought; amongst the Powhatans, he was royalty. A good part of him had wanted to remain with them. But…he was afraid to lose connection to the world he had known, in little things, like mince pies, and large, like music he understood and enjoyed. As for the gifts they'd showered upon him? He'd traded them all away again for more food over the ensuing weeks.

He was at the second village for several days when a growing sense of excitement seized the natives, culminating, in late afternoon, with the arrival of a particular elder whom the others seemed to revere. He was a grim-visaged sort, this elder, who said nothing to Xander and little to anyone else, but nevertheless required the boy to turn in a full circle upon first meeting him, that the elder might view him more fully. That done, Xander stood quietly, awaiting further instructions, when the elder abruptly turned and walked away.

As he was clearly baffled by this exchange, one of Xander's original escorts explained, as best he could, that this elder was the Great Werowance, somehow kin to the late Chief Powhatan, and had determined that Xander should not die. At least, that was Xander's interpretation of things.

That night, the village had a grand feast in honor of this visiting elder, a feast at which Xander had the most diverse and complete meal he'd eaten in memory. There was all manner of meat, of course, including venison, several varieties of fowl, beaver, rabbit, woodchuck, turtle, snake, and more kinds of fish than Xander could recall. Along with this, though, were shoots, tubers, berries, and several larger, stranger fruits that were all delicious, their appearance notwithstanding. These, of course, were of great interest to Will, who wondered if Xander could find some nearby that they might be cultivated. To his surprise, Xander produced several seeds wrapped in leaves from inside his jerkin.

Having interrupted the boy's tale, Will quickly encouraged him to continue with the details of the feast. There was singing, Xander said, after a fashion, and dancing, too. There were also tales, of which he understood nary a word, and even pranks and jests, so that the whole evening was more festive than any Xander had ever experienced.

In time, many of the natives returned to their separate huts, while others fell asleep by the fire. At one point, Xander looked up and the Great Werowance was gone, along with his personal bodyguard, though whether this was simply off to bed or out of the village entirely, he was never to learn, for the man was nowhere to be seen when the boy rose mid-morning of the following day.

Will interjected at this point in the tale, his curiosity getting the better of him at last. What did Xander do all day with his hosts—or were they captors? Had he interacted with the Powhatan youth? What were the women like? And how was the wilderness at night? Did he or his hosts feel no fear of the surrounding darkness? Had Xander seen any other sorts of natives during his time away? How much of the Powhatan language had he learned?

The boy was overwhelmed by this barrage of questions, but managed, gradually, to answer most of them. Nighttime, he said, was frightening at first, as the fields and forests fairly sang with the cries and calls of unfamiliar birds and beasts. Every sound seemed a threat, initially, until Xander noticed his hosts were not the least discomforted. Put them all in Southwark, though, and their positions would be reversed, he knew, because he recognized and understood the meaning behind every little noise at home, whereas the natives would be lost. So it was for him in this great wilderness, home to these Powhatans.

Xander answered the rest of his father's questions until his voice was raw with overuse, but the man's curiosity was insatiable. The only way to divert him, Xander knew, was to get him talking.

"Do you know any stories?" the boy asked.

"Do I know any stories?" Will almost shouted in disbelief. "Does a bear shit in the woods?"

"I've seen a lot of bear shit recently."

"No doubt, no doubt," Will grinned. "And would you have me tell a story, then?"

Xander nodded.

"Very well. Let me see...There once was a great duke, one Prospero by name, who, with his infant daughter, was cast asea by a treacherous brother..."

Will's story lasted until every conceivable chore was done and the property was in as fine a state as ever they'd seen it. Soon, too, the palisade would be complete, allowing Will to focus on making his new home not just self-contained but self-sufficient, requiring fewer trips into town and less interaction with his fellow settlers. For he was otherwise strangely satisfied, was Will. In Margaret, he had a companion who shared and understood the passions of his former life; in young Alexander, he had another, final chance at being a father worthy of the title. He thought briefly, then, of his daughters and resolved to do better, to *be* better, so that to be or not to be was not the question after all, but *how* to be. How to be was really the only choice offered any of us, he thought, and so many do not realize this until it is too late.

This line of thinking naturally made him ponder death, his own death, and especially the first one.

~ 22 ~

A Friend Should Bear
His Friend's Infirmities

Stratford-upon-Avon, March, 1613

It was all Ben's idea, of course. But Will hadn't done much to resist.

They'd been drinking, and Will had been complaining—'whining,' Ben called it—about his life.

"If you don't like the direction in which this play is headed, you'd best rewrite the script!" he'd said.

"That's easy for you to say," Will had countered weakly. "Coming up with a viable plan is harder than it looks."

"When did you become such a dullard? The old Will was never at a loss for ideas on how to advance the plot. If anything, you had too many ideas."

"What would you have me do, kill someone?" Will smirked.

A disconcerting sparkle came to Ben's eyes, then. "Yes! Why not?"

"And who," Will asked with barely contained exasperation, "is the hapless jackanapes to be?"

"You!"

"Me? That's your grand solution? I should kill myself?"

Ben took a prodigious gulp of his beer, exhaled, and answered, "You misunderstand me. You should kill William Shakespeare, give the poor fellow a funeral, and then sneak off for—oh, I don't know—France?"

Will paused with his own beer halfway to his mouth. "That," said he, "is not the most implausible thing I've ever heard from you. But what shall I do for a body? One that will fool my wife and daughters?"

"We could say you were horribly burnt in an accident. That would allow for a closed casket."

"Or..." Will said, "I could die of something catching, and they'll just bury me in a shroud. No one will be able to see that my face is, well, not my face. We lack only a corpse."

"That is not a problem that cannot be solved with coin."

"Yes, and it might be I can get John to play his old doctor one last time."

"John?" Ben asked.

"Heminges. I'll need someone to manage my monies, at all events, and he's as likely a man as any."

Ben appeared much taken aback. "You don't think me worthy of the task?"

Now, it was Will's turn to laugh. "I trust you to kill me, sir. That should be enough for you."

Ben sat back, disappointed. Anon, he said, "When shall we do this thing? The Ides of March?"

Will shook his head. "No. I'll need more time than that to get everything in order. How about my birthday? There's a certain symmetry to it."

"Your birthday?" Ben chortled. "You're a sick man, Will Shakespeare, but that's what I like about you."

The dead man Ben procured for the purpose was a good four inches taller than Will and missing his right foot, necessitating the acquisition of another to take its place. Sadly, spare feet were in short supply that week, and the conspirators had to make due with a left. From a woman.

"Excellent!" Ben declared, when they'd attached the foot with some rough cordage and packed the legs into stockings.

"But he's got two left feet!" Will protested.

"Say that again?"

"He's got two left feet!"

"That has a certain ring to it, don't you think?"

"And one's the wrong size!" Will growled, shaking his head in irritation. "I'm glad you find all of this so amusing. Perhaps one day I can return the favor."

By previous arrangement with their favorite tapster, they stashed the dead man in a storage room of his tavern. Will and Ben then stayed, drinking, until well after closing. When the moment arrived, Will stripped down and they dressed the corpse in his clothing. It was only when Ben asked his friend to turn over his jewelry so it might be given to his wife that Will began to have second thoughts.

"Come on, now, Hamlet. 'Tis time to strike," Ben goaded.

"Yes," Will sighed. "But what if..."

"What if? What if? What if this turns out well? What if you meet a new woman and fall helplessly, hopelessly in love? What if she gives you a brood of fine fellows? Do or do not. Audere est faucere."

With a sour frown, Will relinquished his rings. "Faber est suae quisque fortunae.

As a final touch, they wrapped the dead man in a burial shroud, with just enough holes in just the right places to expose bits of Will's clothing."

"I'll tell your wife and daughters you were sick with fever, shaking, and coughing up bits of lung."

"Don't lay it on too thick," Will warned.

"I know what I'm doing," said Ben. "I'm England's greatest living writer, after all..."

~ 23 ~

THOU ART A SLAVE,
WHOM FORTUNE'S TENDER ARM
WITH FAVOUR NEVER CLASP'D

Jamestown, August, 1619

At long last someone from town came by with the dog Will had requested, a puppy of indeterminate breed (which likely explained its availability—the English being so particular about their dogs). This sparked a days-long debate about what to name it. Margaret favored Dogberry; Will liked Crab, and Xander, Ruffian. Other candidates included Doggerel, Dogma and Doge. In the end, they settled on the unfortunate name of Sir Doggles of Doggington Manor—Sir Doggles, for short. Will had tossed it out there as a lark, and it stuck.

This discussion might have raged for days, though, had not a ship arrived in town, carrying workers from Africa, an event that precipitated a chain of unforeseeable consequences which impacted not only the lives of everyone in Jamestown, but indeed millions yet ungotten and unborn who would have cause to rue the occasion.

For Xander, of course, it was especially frightening.

It was August, and a hotter, stuffier day Will could not remember, not even during his journeys through Italy and Greece. Whatever a man drank was immediately secreted as sweat, so that every gulp seemed a race against deadly thirst, and yet there was only so much fluid one's belly and bladder could hold. Most of the settlers took refuge in the shade, and, a lucky few, in root cellars, which remained comparatively cool year 'round. The Jamieson place had one, too, but it was pitifully small. Will never imagined he'd come to covet a hole in the ground—though he reminded himself again that he was destined for one sooner or later—so he added expansion of the existing one to the list of improvements he planned to make to his homestead.

It was whilst visiting his neighbor across the road and inspecting such a cellar that he first learned of the slaves.

"I was thinking of purchasing one of the Africans offloaded by that Dutch ship the other day."

Will stared at his neighbor as if he'd sprouted a second head. "What do you mean?"

"There was a Dutch ship came to town—or more likely an English ship flyin' Dutch flags to deceive the Spanish—and it sold a number of slaves in trade for water, tobacco and victuals."

"Slaves," said Will, stupidly.

"Well," said Alvah, "servants, they call 'em, but they'll be slaves soon enough, won't they? I daresay you'll be gettin' offers for your apprentice. What's his name, again?"

"Alexander. And he's not for sale."

"I wasn't inquirin'. Just makin' an observation."

"Nevertheless, slaves in the colony?"

Alvah blew out his lips and arched his brows, as if surprised by Will's response. "They are not like us, after all."

"Are they not?" Will countered. "Hath not a slave eyes? Hath not a slave hands, organs, dimensions, senses, affections, passions? Are they not fed with the same food, hurt with the same weapons, subject to the same diseases, healed by the same means, warmed and cooled by the same winter and summer, as an Englishman? If you prick them, do they not bleed? If you tickle them, do they not laugh? If you poison them, do they not die?"

Alvah cocked his head, taken aback and clearly confused by Will's passion. "Is that Scripture, neighbor? I don't...I don't recognize it."

"Leviticus," Will lied, secretly confident the man would race for his Bible as soon as they parted ways. "Well," he added, "You've given me much to think about. I thank you, and I take my leave."

He must have looked most perturbed upon entering the cottage, for Margaret and Xander promptly asked him what was amiss. "We've got slaves in the colony now," said he. "African slaves. And I don't want our young man here mistaken for anyone's property."

"They wouldn't dare!" Margaret exclaimed.

"I'll not wager on it, either way. The time is out of joint."

Margaret sighed. "So it seems—monsters i' the wood, treacherous settlers, changeable natives, the constant threat of Spaniards and now slavery?"

"And to think I was bored back in England."

"Do you regret coming?"

"The man who regrets nothing has never truly lived. I might have been kinder, more honest, more devout. But for coming here? No. My soul sings with the strangeness of it all."

"But will they try to make a slave of me?" Xander asked.

Will recognized the boy's growing distress. "They may try, but trying and doing are of slender acquaintance in such matters. And besides, you have Margaret and myself to protect you—not to mention the brave Sir Doggles," Will smiled. "Surely no man has ever possessed such formidable allies." For a moment, he grew more serious and added, "At all events, I must perforce speak with this House of Burgesses. As Margaret makes clear, far too many threats have gone unanswered. I will press for remedy."

Like so many things in life, this proved easier said than done. The House of Burgesses was comprised of two representatives from each of the eleven settlements that had sprung up in Virginia, including Jamestown. It convened in Jamestown's church, but because its members did not live in Jamestown proper, they could not be summoned on a moment's notice. Thus, it was weeks before Will had his chance to address the assembly, during which interval, virtually all of his problems continued unabated. The locals continued to find evidence of the Wendigo's predations, Will's nameless, faceless assailants continued to hector him and his family, and the Powhatans continued to linger uncomfortably near his home. Were they watching over him? Waiting for an opportunity to raid his cottage? He still had little insight into their ambitions and desires, despite Xander's experience.

For all that, Will's new life was not without its pleasures or its progress. He was quite comfortable with his little family, rather attached to Margaret, Xander and Sir Doggles and had good hope of obtaining a horse, soon. He'd have had one already, he learned, had not the original settlers eaten theirs during the so-called "Starving Time." But a horse would allow for more-frequent visits to town (with a lot less discomfort), more exploration, and even greater productivity in his own farming efforts. He could not plant tobacco right now—that would have to wait for next spring—but a horse would be of enormous help in preparing the field and cultivating the soil. Perhaps he would also purchase a pig or goat. Will didn't want to get too involved in animal husbandry; he still aimed for less labor and more leisure. But he knew livestock was a good investment, and it was always wise to have one's own source for meat. Whereas a man might find whatever he needed in the shops and markets of London or even Stratford, Virginians had to be self-sufficient. And while Will had made great inroads in that direction, he had much still to accomplish.

It had been raining since the middle of the night, and a serious, motivated rain it was. The kind that trapped a person indoors for the duration, hoping the firewood would hold out until the worst had passed.

Will stood at a window on the leeward side of the cottage, gazing at the downpour through a partially-opened shutter, puffing the smoke from his pipe out into the air. Through the white noise of rainfall, a particular rhythm caught his attention— an on-going double-drip in the closest rain barrel that went blip BLOP blip BLOP blip BLOP. Iambs. And, of course, it followed that he could not hear them without assigning words: *If music be the food of love, play on!* There was a local bird, whose name he had yet to learn, that spoke in dactyls. And he'd heard various rhythms from Virginia's frogs, from trochees to anapests. There was, he supposed, an entire canon to be enjoyed, if a man could but make sense of it. The comedies and romances he could well imagine, but the tragedies and histories? Who were nature's heroes and villains? For the frog ate the grasshopper, and the snake ate the frog, and the owl ate the snake, and the fox ate the owl...It was all a matter of perspective, really. Who could say, but that this Grendel was the hero of nature's tale, and the settlers were its villains? It might be that Grendel was nature's way of telling the colonists to leave the New World. But men—and Englishmen in particular—had never been good at heeding warnings. No; they wanted what they wanted, and damn the consequences.

It was a form of violence, is what it was.

Will frowned and closed the shutters. He hated such thoughts. There was nothing but untold miles of wilderness in every direction. Surely, this land could accommodate a few thousand—even a few hundred thousand—settlers. What was the harm in turning meadows into fields of tobacco? Why should nature prefer one plant over another?

Or one man?

Which thought, of course, brought him back to the Africans and the Powhatans.

He was suffering a bout of what he called "frantic brain," in which his own thoughts were like to drive him mad if he could not distract himself. Fleetingly, he thought of his opium and immediately scolded himself. A cup or bottle of wine might do the trick, though. Or a nap. Perhaps he could convince Margaret to play upon the lute...

~ 24 ~

SMOOTH RUNS THE WATER
WHERE THE BROOK IS DEEP;
AND IN HIS SIMPLE SHOW
HE HARBOURS TREASON.

Jamestown, September, 1619

One afternoon, as August gave way to September, the whole family sat under the yard's lone tree, near the palisade, basking in the shade and enjoying an unexpectedly refreshing breeze. Margaret sat on a blanket spread across the grass, struck up a chord upon Will's ancient lute, and began to sing.

It was a lover and his lass
With a hey, and a ho, and a hey nonino,
That o'er the green cornfield did pass,
In springtime, the only pretty ring time,
When birds do sing, hey ding a ding, ding;
Sweet lovers love the spring…

"I know this one!" Xander exclaimed, after Margaret had finished.

"Canst sing, boy?" Will asked.

Without another word, Xander launched into song, whilst the lady struggled to keep up on the lute.

Pastime with good company
I love and shall until' I die
Grudge who lust, but none deny

So God be pleased, thus live will I
For my pastance,
Hunt sing and dance
My heart is set
All goodly sport,
To my comfort
Who shall me let?...

"Well done!" said Will. "Well done!"

"And now, I believe it is your turn," Margaret prodded him.

"Hmmm. Let me see, let me see. Do you know Johnny Be Fine?"

"Oh, pish!" said Margaret, "And I do not, let me forsake my maiden's weeds and live out my life as a man!" Whereupon she began to play a most lively tune.

Will cleared his throat and began.

Oh Johnny be fine and Johnny be fair and wants me for to wed.
And I would marry Johnny but me father up and said
I'm sorry to tell you daughter, what your mother never knew,
But Johnny is a son of mine and so is kin to you.

Oh Thomas be fine and Thomas be fair and wants me for to wed.
And I would marry Thomas but me father up and said

I'm sorry to tell you daughter, what your mother never knew,
But Thomas is a son of mine and so is kin to you.

Oh Daniel be fine and Daniel be fair and wants me for to wed.
And I would marry Daniel but me father up and said

I'm sorry to tell you daughter, what your mother never knew,
But Daniel is a son of mine and so is kin to you.

O you never saw a maid so sad and sorry as I was.
The lads in town are all my kin and me father is the cause.
If life should thus continue I should die a single miss
I think I'll go to mother and complain to her of this.

O daughter didn't I tell you to forgive and to forget?
Your father sowed his wild oats, but still you need not fret
Your father may be father to all the lads but still
He's not the one who sired you so marry who you will.

The laughter that followed Will's efforts was one of the great highlights of his time in the New World, he concluded, and he felt no desire to move from his seat beneath the tree for the rest of the day. Sensing this, Margaret went into the cottage and returned with a meal of bread, cheese, dried meat, fruit and wine. Sir Doggles came and lay down next to Alexander and made no secret of his interest in the boy's victuals. Oh, he was a shameless beggar, was Sir Doggles, but an exceptional companion nonetheless, and his antics made the day merrier still. Will couldn't remember when he'd last been so content. Thoughts from his previous life tried to intrude upon his reverie, to spoil his moment with guilt, but he held fast to the instant. There would be time for such concerns later, he knew, as he tried to sleep or struggled with his bowels in the jakes. But he would grant them no audience now, not so much as a keyhole through which to eavesdrop upon his happiness. He had earned it and paid for it, too.

It was not long before the wine and the shivering of leaves in the breeze conspired against him and lured him into a slumber. In time, the heat of the day proved too much for him, and he roused himself and went into the cottage, where it was slightly cooler.

"At last, I understand why the natives dress as they do!" he gasped. "This heat's like to boil the fat right off me. Enough to keep the town's lanterns burning for weeks."

The very idea launched young Xander into an attack of the giggles.

"You laugh," said Will, "who have no fat to speak of. If to be fat is to be hated, then Pharoah's lean kine are to be loved."

"What is kine?"

"*Are* kine," Will corrected. "What are kine?"

"Arcane," Margaret added.

"Abstain," said Will.

"Bloodstain."

"Again," Xander offered, catching on to this new game.

"Sustain."

"Legerdemain," Will called out triumphantly.

"Military campaign?" Margaret asked.

"No, madam. That's two words!

"Can we play again?" Xander wanted to know.

Will looked at the young man and placed a hand on his shoulder. "Ever and always, Alexander. A man of words is never alone, unarmed or ill-equipped. Now," he added, "help me out of these infernal boots—unless you'd like roasted toes for dinner." That task accomplished, Will proceeded to strip down to his undergarments, saying, "Given the choice of embarrassing you two or dying of this damnable heat, well, you see where I stand."

"Or not," said Margaret, with a wicked glint in her eyes.

Now, Will was the one embarrassed. "Uh, yes. In any case, I'm off to sit in the brook 'til winter comes."

"You'll take your pistol?"

"I'll go with you," Xander said.

"Excellent," said Will, as he grabbed his flintlock and headed out the door. "And bring that ruffian, Sir Doggles."

It was like stepping into a foundry, so oppressive was the heat.

"Fuck!" Will spat, at which Xander giggled anew. "What? Don't tell me you never heard anyone swear at Lucy's place."

"Oh, aye, that I have. I just never expected such from you, bein' a *man of words* and all."

"Last I checked, 'fuck' was a word. And an old one, too. Probably older than many a building in London, for that matter."

"Then why don't you curse more often?" Xander wanted to know.

"I curse constantly, it's just that the words seldom make it past my lips. And, until recently, I had a reputation to uphold. Now, however, I am blissfully free to say 'fuck, it's hot' all I want."

Xander nodded in agreement. "Hottest place I've ever been."

"Let's hope the stream hasn't evaporated."

It had not. Reaching its banks at last, Will wasted no time in plopping himself down in the nearest eddy, while Xander sat on a rock in the shade and dangled his feet into the current.

"Poseidon be praised," said Will. "And if I have to live in this little pool until autumn's come and gone, I'll do't." His gaze softened and he seemed to daydream for a moment, before he added, "There is a willow grows aslant a brook..."

"Yes?" Xander prompted, hoping, perhaps, for another tale.

Will was lost in thought, though, and said nothing further for some time.

Xander became bored and began wading downstream with Sir Doggles in tow. Suddenly, he shot his hands into the water and came out holding a crayfish, a huge smile stretching across his face.

The dog barked and barked at the thing as if it were a monster.

"What's that you've got there, boy?"

"I don't know what it's called," Xander replied, crossing over to Will in order to show him.

"Ah. Crayfish."

"Crayfish."

"Yes," Will said. "You can eat them."

"Are they good?"

"I like them. We ate them all the time where I grew up."

"Maybe I'll catch more for supper?"

"Well bethought!" Will smiled back at the young man. There was no harm in encouraging him, and if he caught enough, it would make a nice change from their usual diet.

With an imp-like cackle, Xander charged off downstream, eager to continue the hunt, to Sir Doggle's beyond-evident delight. Will scooped water onto his bald pate with both hands and closed his eyes, the better to enjoy the sensation. In the next instant, however, he heard Xander cry out and Will stumbled to his feet in alarm.

"What is it?" he called out, retrieving his pistol from the nearest stone.

"Bones!" Xander called back. "A man's bones, I think."

Will felt his heart pounding in his chest like Hephaestus at the anvil, but at least Xander was not in peril. For the moment. In twenty-some strides, he gained Xander's side and stared down into the water, where part of a ribcage and skull lay half-submerged in the mud of the stream bottom. Farther downstream, Will spied larger bones...in smaller pieces.

"Run and fetch Margaret, would you?" He asked his son. "And tell her to bring a spade and a large sack."

Xander looked torn for a moment, unsure what to do with his prize, but also fully invested in this new mystery. With a shrug, he dropped the crayfish back into the stream and bolted for the cottage.

When Xander returned with Margaret, Will said, "First things first: you can still hunt for crayfish, lad, but only upstream of where I was bathing. We don't want to eat of anything that consumed our friend here." He gestured to the bones before going on. "Second, I'll pull the bones, wash them in the creek, and Margaret, if you'd be so kind, will lay them out in the sun, just beyond the tree line."

Normally up for any kind of adventure, Margaret made a face, instead. "Hadn't we better bury it?"

"And we shall, good my mouse of virtue. But first, I'd like to know what we have here. A man? A woman? A settler, or one of the natives? A victim of war or of our Grendel?"

"I thought we were calling him Caliban. Or was it Wendigo?"

"It's Grendel now, and there an end on't."

"And what shall I do?" Xander inquired.

"We need a lookout man," Will told him, "that none of our numerous enemies comes upon us unawares."

Xander wasn't happy with that answer, but he scratched Sir Doggles behind the ears and kept his disappointment to himself.

Without another word, Will bent to the stream and began jiggling and pulling at the skeleton's ribcage as gently but firmly as possible. And, little by little, he succeeded in extracting the various pieces. Gone was Will's worry about the heat, gone, too, was any thought of preparing the evening meal. In an hour's time, he had the pelvis, spine, ribcage, scapulae and clavicles drying in the sun in their correct positions, more or less.

"I could use your help now, son," a winded Will exclaimed.

Xander looked over, excited.

"I'm still missing the majority of the skull, the arms, the legs, hands and feet." He pointed out the bits of femur in the mud downstream.

As Xander raced into action, Will joined Margaret at the skeleton. On creaking knees, he knelt down and took hold of one of the scapulae.

"Our friend here was shot. See this hole?" He stuck a finger through it and wiggled it around for Margaret's benefit. He then leaned down and pointed at the pieces of corresponding clavicle. "And see here? Completely obliterated. Just these two fragments. That's the exit wound. In the back, out the front."

"Shot in the back. But why are the arms and legs not with the body?"

Will shrugged. "Wolves? Bears?"

"Or Grendel."

"Yes," Will agreed. "Or Grendel."

"But why tear the arms and legs off? For the marrow?"

"That's my thought," Will answered.

Margaret grimaced at the bones. "And the skull was most likely taken for the brain, yes?"

"Then he can't have been a gentleman..."

In another half hour, they'd assembled the skeleton entire. The skull, from all Will could tell, had been bitten in half, confirming the group's theory that something had eaten the brain and, thus, the corpse. But questions remained. Was the victim male or female? Settler or native? Where were its clothes? Why had he or she been shot? Had the victim been dragged here from elsewhere by the monster, or had the poor soul died here, too?

Will placed most of the bones in the bag, except for the gunshot scapula and the two major pieces of the skull.

Margaret asked, "What do you intend with those?"

"I'll show them to Sir George. He'll know if anyone's gone

missing from the village," Will responded. To Xander, he said, "Would you scout a bit farther downstream and up? If there be any more bodies, we'd best know now. But, look you, stay within hailing distance. I'd not lose you again, young sir, for anything."

This last comment brought an enormous smile to the lad's face, and he raced off with alacrity. Will watched him go for a moment, before turning his attention to the nearby underbrush.

"Be damned," he said, "if it isn't Robin-Run-the-Hedge!"

Utterly baffled, Margaret said, "What?"

"This plant here, this weed. It's Robin-Run-the-Hedge. We used to pick this as children to stuff mattresses or to torment each other with its stickiness."

"And how is this related to our dead man?"

"Not at all," Will confessed. "It's just oddly comforting to see a piece of home so far from it…"

"Regretting your choice?" Margaret asked for the hundredth time.

Will's face acquired the most bittersweet expression she'd ever seen from him. "Regrets are false portents of things that never were. Here, now, I have a home, and I hope it feels so to you, too."

Margaret reached out and took his arm. "It feels silly to say, given everything we've endured thus far, but I have never felt safer or more appreciated."

Sometimes the best thing a man of words can say is nothing at all, understanding that the language of love is made of something more, something ineffable, that cannot, will not be quantified. And so, Will was content to stand with Margaret, gazing off towards the stream and savoring a moment of relative tranquility. Soon, Xander came rushing back to them, barely winded, looking fresher than spring itself.

"Nothing," said he.

Will sighed with conspicuous relief. "Very good. We'll stash these bones for later burial, once we've identified their owner. These other bits I'll take into town tomorrow."

"And what shall we call this stream?" Xander asked.

Before Will could answer, Margaret said, "I propose we call it Xander's Run."

"Xander's Run!" Will repeated. "I like it!"

"Xander's Run!" said the boy, clearly delighted with the name.

Sir Doggles barked enthusiastically, presumably in agreement.

~ 25 ~

TALKING ISN'T DOING

Jamestown, September, 1619

By happy circumstance, Will arrived in town the next day whilst a gathering of the House of Burgesses was still in session and managed to garner himself an audience with the same. The assembly took place in the church and, upon entering, he was heckled by one of the locals.

"Didn't know you were able to enter a church, Master Kemp!"

"Or you, a school. But the world is full of surprises, good neighbor, is it not?"

The inside of Jamestown's church was stiflingly hot, rather like the hell it purported to save its parishioners from suffering. The assembly needed space and privacy—Will understood that— but he'd have thought a forest glen more suitable in such heat.

Sir George noticed him the moment he entered and waved him over, whereupon the governor introduced him to his deputy and the colony's treasurer, Sir Edwin Sandys, reminding Will that Jamestown was very much still a business venture of the Virginia Company, and they expected to return a profit on their investment. And the monied were not known for their patience. In addition to Sir George and his administration, there were a scribe, twenty-two representatives from the eleven little towns that had grown from the initial colony, and a small number of others who remained unidentified.

"Gentlemen," Sir George called out loudly, "may I present to you Master William Kemp, late of…"

"Warwickshire," Will offered.

"Warwickshire, and now one of our more august citizens."

"Well read, well-bred and well fed, as the saying goes," said Will.

"You bought the Jamison place!" one of the others observed.

"I did."

"A fortuitous purchase," another added. "It's a marvelous property."

"And," Sir George cut in, "Will has taken great pains to improve upon it."

Uncomfortable with this focus on his wealth, Will changed the subject. "I wished to address you all today, if I may, on the subject of this creature that threatens our safety."

"Does it, though?" asked a fat man with his hair sweat-plastered across his brow.

"It more than threatened the Jamiesons, and I am certain their spirits cry out for vengeance, for justice."

"That's as may be," another man said dryly. "I see no reason I should be the one to provide it, living as far from this place as anyone in Virginia. This beast is unlikely to bother me and mine, and I have more than enough concerns of my own."

Will studied the man for a few heartbeats. He was a gaunt, dour fellow, with a high forehead, a long, sharp nose, and catastrophically thin lips. If a man could be judged by his countenance alone, this one was as severe and ungenerous of spirit as any Will had met thus far. Knowing an appeal to the man's conscience would yield him little, he tried a different approach.

"I was under the impression these colonies were part of a larger business venture by the Virginia Company. Surely, they won't be pleased when this creature's predations lead to reduced immigration and commerce."

The assembly erupted into agreements, contradictions and all manner of commentary until Sir George raised his voice and demanded silence.

The fat man said, "But we've just brought in some ninety marriageable women! That can only be to our good."

"Perhaps," said Will, "we should halt new arrivals until

we've captured this monster. Unless, of course, you cherish the idea of more dead."

The dour man jumped into the fray again. "You're assuming there's only one of these beasts!"

"All the more reason for us to band together and kill it, or them, before they kill us." Will countered. Round and round the debate went, until it became clear the assembly would be of no help in the matter. Finally, Will relented. "I am sorry to see that amongst our country's many contributions to this New World, bureaucracy seems to be in the forefront. I bid you good day, gentlemen." With that, he bowed and made his way outside, where, though it was still warm, at least there was a gentle breeze and the scent of things other than sweat and stale breath. To his surprise, Sir George had followed him out.

"As you can see," he said without preamble, "I've quite the task ahead of me."

Will nodded. "I do not envy you, sir. More will die because of this creature."

"We haven't seen any new evidence of it in a while now..."

"No?" Will produced the scapula and part of the skull he'd been keeping in his pockets.

The governor said nothing, but held his hands out, that he might examine the fragments himself.

"My little family and I found the skeleton entire. Looks to have been shot in the back, but the shooter, surely, did not then devour the brain. And these bones aren't weathered enough to date to the Starving Time."

Sir George winced at this reference to the colony's most infamous period. "No," he agreed.

"The question is, has anyone disappeared in the last six months or so? And why was that person shot and by whom?"

"What manner of clothing was our victim wearing?"

"We found none."

The governor's eyebrows shot up almost comically. "I'm afraid you've opened Pandora's Box, Master Kemp. These bones suggest we have both a murderer and a monster in our midst."

"Not to mention the villains who assaulted my lady friend and me."

Sir George regarded him with a gimlet eye. "Mention it, you did though. And I say again that I am actively investigating."

Again, Will changed the subject, sensing he'd gone as far as he could on the previous topics. "Is it always so *warm* in summers here?"

The governor chuckled and sleeved his brow. "Lucky fellow that you are, Master Kemp, you've arrived for the worst of it. I'm told this is the hottest summer we've had since the colony was founded. I'll wager you won't see its like for years to come."

"Well, that's a blessing, at least."

Will was on his way to the little market when he ran into his neighbor, Alvah. He tried to pretend he hadn't seen the man, but Alvah, clearly, had something he wished to discuss.

"So, you *can* go into a church," said he.

"And what is that, the daily quip? Is it posted somewhere hereabouts?"

Momentarily taken aback by Will's manner, Alvah struggled to proceed. "I, eh, I were just wondering if you'd heard about Chapman's horse."

Will sighed and fanned himself with his hat. "I have not. Who is Chapman?"

"Our neighbor to the west."

"Ah. We haven't met."

"Well, his horse was killed last night. Eaten, it seems."

Eaten. "I'm guessing you don't mean to say it was eaten by Chapman..."

"No," Alvah confirmed. "Nor even by the savages."

"Because?"

"All Chapman found when he searched his pasture were the horse's hooves and tail."

"Very well, sir," Will said at last, "since you seem to want my thoughts on this matter, I believe this is more of our monster's doing. I have raised this issue with the House of Burgesses, and it appears we're on our own in this fight." Tired of the man's company, Will asked, "Was there anything else, Alvah?"

"Since you're askin'," Alvah responded, "I've been wonderin' about your mistress."

Ah. Here it was. "Yes?"

"She's an odd one, isn't she?"

"How so?"

"Well, she's not exactly...I mean to say, she's not really a woman, is she?"

"Isn't she?" Will gasped, feigning shocked innocence as if he were still being paid to perform.

"Look at her! Broad-shouldered, fighting a beard, no breasts to speak of."

"Nonsense!" Will said. "The same could be said of my granddam."

"You know what I mean."

"Do I, though?"

Exasperated, Alvah said, "If there's no cock beneath those weeds, I'll eat my bible."

"Do you hear yourself, sir? It's a strange obsession you've got there."

"It's no obsession!" Alvah spat, growing red-faced. "And I'm not the one sharing a roof with her. At the very least."

"Alas," Will said. "You've found me out. Naught but endless orgies and sodomy at my place. The boy's involved, too. And the dog! We do nothing all day but wallow in filth and damnation, sir. Wallow, I say!" When he was done laughing, Will looked up to find Alvah had gone.

The storage building-cum-market had a few new items on its shelves—foodstuffs and household items that must have arrived with the aforementioned shipment of women—things Will was only too happy to snap up for himself and his housemates. There was also, to his surprise, a package in his name that had just come in as well. Inside the package was a small sculpture of a globe, the world. The sphere itself seemed to be hollow, but the base was quite heavy, which instantly made Will suspicious. Examining it more closely, he could see that it had been signed "Heminges." Hidden inside the base, then, was a message from his business partner back in London, if not, in fact, a portion of his latest profits. While he was not close to being low on funds, every little bit helped.

He stopped by the brewery and sampled the tapster's latest effort, too, and was pleased to discover it was not as vile as the previous. In fact, it was almost palatable. Nothing to savor over an evening meal, of course, but serviceable for breakfast and lunch. If the water in Xander's Run—upstream of the skeleton, of course—wasn't among the sweetest, most refreshing Will had ever tasted, he might have felt compelled to order a small cask or two. As it was, the wines and ale he'd brought from England were still in sufficient supply that he could avoid the local brew until the tapster perfected its making—or died trying. Then, too, there were others in the colony who made their own beer. Perhaps the governor would be willing to sponsor a friendly contest to determine who made the best, whereupon Will could make the winner an offer for, say, half his supply.

The town seemed livelier today than at any point in memory. Will supposed this was due to the presence of the men of the House of Burgesses, combined with the recent influx of women. Whatever the case, he found it much easier to hail a ride back to his homestead. An affable young fellow with his own horse and wagon offered him a ride and even helped to pull Will up onto the driver's bench.

"William Kemp," Will said by way of introduction.

"Robert Skinner,' the young man replied.

"I've not seen you before, have I?"

"I doubt it," said Robert. "I live a ways east of here, towards the coast. I'm only in town once or twice a season to trade and catch up on the news. But you are new to me, as well."

"It's true. I arrived on the George in April and purchased the Jamieson place."

"Brave man!" said Robert. "I hear they were eaten by bears or massacred by these savage natives."

Having expounded at some length on the nature of rumor in his previous life, Will considered his companion's comment a moment before answering, "Rumor is like gonorrhea, ill-spread and unhealthy. No, my predecessors were killed by something else. Have you had no mysterious murders or disappearances in your settlement?"

"Not a one. What is it you think killed the Jamiesons, then?"

Will studied his new friend for several seconds and then said, "Have you ever seen an ape, Master Skinner?"

"Images only. And you?"

"I have. In the bear-baiting pits in London, I once saw an ape—a huge, black thing, it was—set upon by a pack of dogs, six or seven in all, I think. The ape won, but bled out shortly thereafter."

"Do you think this was an ape?"

"'Tis something like, but also like a bear and somewhat like a wolf. All three and none of 'em."

"A new beast."

Will nodded. "New to us, perhaps. And then again, perhaps not. Does the word 'Wendigo' mean anything to you?"

Robert shook his head.

"It's the natives' name for this creature."

From the look on Robert's face, it was clear he was trying to be amicable but did not entirely credit Will's story. "Have you seen this thing?"

"I have not," said Will. "But I've seen its footprints and handprints often enough."

"Begging your pardon, sir, but has anyone else seen these prints?"

"Oh, aye. My lady-friend has seen them, too."

"You called them 'handprints'."

"So I did, and so they are. But giant hands with enormous, terrible claws."

"But not a bear's…"

"Bears do not have fingers."

Somehow, over the last mile or so, Robert had begun to believe, for he scanned the woods on either side of the path as surreptitiously as possible. With studied nonchalance, he asked, "If such a thing exists, why haven't the people of Jamestown found and killed it?"

"A question I've asked many times. In sooth, I've just addressed the House of Burgesses on the matter, but none of its members seem inclined to pursue it."

"What will you do?"

Will leaned back on the bench, stretched. "Though I be

passenger on your cart, Master Skinner, I am captain of my destiny, and the counsel will not solve my problem, I must of force."

There was a prolonged lull in the conversation, until Will spoke again. He wanted to know what to expect of autumn in Virginia and after that, of course, winter. Winter, it turned out, was a favorite subject of Robert's, for he loved, of all things, to fish and to play upon the frozen rivers when the air was cold enough. To Will, this sounded like the perfect method for self-injury, but Robert laughed off his concerns. Young bones, young bones. But it was impossible not to like the young man, and by the time they reached the edge of Will's property, it was as if they'd been friends forever.

"You're welcome to dinner, sir!" Will said. "I daresay my apprentice would relish your company."

Robert tipped his cap and begged off, having still too much to accomplish before he headed back to his own lands, though he did promise to return at the soonest opportunity.

When Will entered the cottage, Margaret was hard at work on her bread, whilst Xander was poring through Beowulf again, sounding out words and trying his best to make sense of it. Out of his satchel, Will produced the things he'd purchased in town and set them on the table, so that the mistress of the house might stash them in their proper places. He had learned, had Will, that Margaret had a very particular system for the placement and storage of various items, and woe betide the man who violated that system. The globe, he set in the center of the table.

"What's that?" Xander asked.

"A silly trinket. But I think there's treasure hidden within its base."

Xander could barely contain his excitement. "Can I get it out for you?"

"Can you do it without injuring yourself?"

The boy snorted, as if the idea of him hurting himself was beyond ludicrous. In seconds, he was hard at work on the task.

Will stepped into his bedroom to strip off his doublet and boots and then returned to the main room to plop himself down in his chair. The moment his bottom hit the seat, Margaret placed a large cup of diluted beer at his elbow.

"Many thanks!" Said Will.

Naturally, both Margaret and Xander demanded a full accounting of his adventures in Jamestown, with character voices where appropriate. Will was sorry to report there was little progress on the identity of the men who had terrorized them and sorrier still to confess that finding and killing their Grendel was of little to no importance to the colony. One day, Will felt certain, they would have cause to rue their indifference. Between now and then, however, he and his might suffer. Unless he acted preemptively.

Pushing these thoughts aside, his eyes fell upon Xander and he was instantly transported, in memory, to an earlier time aboard the ship.

~ 26 ~

THE WHORESON MUST BE ACKNOWLEDGED

London, April, 1619

Most of the passengers cycled through the galley in shifts. It was a small, tight space and offered no comfort or privacy whatsoever. Will, having paid a hefty sum for his passage and Xander's, was allowed to take his meals in his cabin. On one such occasion as the two ate, mired in their thoughts, Xander broke the silence.

"How did you know my mother?"

The question was so unexpected that it took Will a moment to answer. "I heard of her before I met her, and, having heard, *had* to meet her."

Xander winced, as if the reply was too precious by half. "And what was she to you?"

"What was she not? My heart, my harbor, my home."

"And yet I never saw you 'til she died."

Will put his meal aside and hung his head. "To my everlasting regret."

"Do you always talk like this?"

"Only when I'm awake," Will responded.

"So you're, what, a poet?"

"I've been called worse. You don't care for poetry?"

"I don't care for poets."

Was he speaking of his mother's many suitors, or of the profession as a whole? "There are some bad ones, I grant you."

"Why write silly lines of nonsense when you could be out doing and being something better?" Xander demanded.

"Such as?"

"Becoming a soldier," Xander said. "Owning an inn. Learning to smith metal."

Of course, it stung that the boy thought being a tapster was of more importance than being a poet—as Xander had intended, Will thought. Rather than engage, he parried, "And which of those appeals most to you?"

"I want to be an assassin."

Oh wonderful son, that can so 'stonish a father. Will was silent.

"Did my mother love you?" Xander pressed, in what was increasingly becoming more fencing match than conversation.

"I think she did."

"Why?"

Will blinked his eyes like a great owl, briefly at a loss for words. "Well," said he, "why does anyone love another? I appreciated her mind, valued her opinion, treasured her sense of humor..."

"Coveted her body."

In a flash, Will rose to his feet, his arm drawn back and ready to strike the boy across the face. Xander watched him, bracing for the expected blow, but did not retreat or back down.

"Do you deny it?" he challenged.

"She was your mother, minnow, and I will not allow you or anyone to disparage her in my presence.

"Disparage?"

"To insult," Will explained, "belittle, or malign."

Xander bobbed his head in understanding. "So, you *did* love her."

"I did and do."

"Why, then, did you leave her? Or if she left you, why didn't you fight for her?" Xander demanded.

"Because your mother never needed rescuing. Because I was a coward. And a thousand reasons more, and not a one of 'em equal to the task, singly or collectively. Damn it, boy, d'you think I would not give my right arm to have her here with us tonight?"

Without warning, Xander began to weep. "Me, too," he said. "Me, too," for he was still a boy, for all his size, his wit, his bluster; he was still a boy as other boys are, and Will promised himself he'd remember that in the future.

~ 27 ~

WHERE TWO RAGING FIRES MEET

The Jamieson Place, September, 1619

It was one of those nights when heat makes sleep impossible, when lying in bed means struggling in sweat-sodden clothing to find a comfortable position on an increasingly damp mattress. Will was not one for sleeping in the nude, but he was out of patience or other ideas. He was just about to rise and strip down when a horrible squealing shattered the otherwise stifling silence. So bad, so prolonged was it, that even Margaret and Xander rose from their own miserable slumbers to listen. In no time, all three stood listening at Will's bedroom shutters.

The squealing became louder and worse, clearly a neighbor's hog in its death throes. Smaller, higher-pitched squeals added to the hurly-burly, only to be joined seconds later by the sound of a man yelling. Next, a musket blast shook the night, followed by a terrible roar and then a scream of mortal agony. Such was the progression and specificity of noises that it was quite clear to the listeners what was transpiring.

Will, having no interest in a repeat catastrophe at his home, turned to Xander and said, "Be a good lad and check all the windows and doors. Margaret, fetch the guns, will you?"

Now, a woman's scream and that of a younger male joined the frightful din, whilst the roaring continued unabated.

Xander, returned from his task, said, "It's the monster, isn't it? Wendigo?"

Will grimaced in the affirmative. "Let's keep our own voices low, shall we? No sense in reminding the beast that we're just across the way."

There was no difficulty in keeping Sir Doggles silent, for he cowered under the table like a beast born to the manner.

"That poor, poor family," Margaret breathed, pushing the musket into Will's hand while she kept the pistol. "But we haven't got a weapon for Xander."

The young man raised his poniard so both adults could see it. "If it comes near me, I'll destroy both its knees."

Meanwhile, the carnage across the road continued, despite the fact that the death cries of Will's neighbors grew weaker and weaker, as the rest of Alvah's livestock went to it. And being limited to hearing-only somehow made things worse, more horrific, as imagination preyed upon Will and the others. This nightmare seemed to stretch on for hours, until at last there was nothing remaining but the sound of snapping.

"What is that?" Xander inquired.

"It sounds like...smells like..."

"Fire," said Margaret.

A new kind of fear seized the trio then, for fire was every bit as voracious, as merciless and unyielding as Grendel and could easily destroy their home.

A little fire is quickly trodden out,
Which being suffered, rivers cannot quench.

Spying Heminges' still-unsolved offering on the table, Will reflected that the world was a globe, and the Globe was a world. His world. And fire had eaten it. Only the death of his son had been more painful, for a theater could be rebuilt. And yet that fire had taken so many of his plays, his poems, his errant scribblings. Beloved manuscripts and things he'd still been working on. Even love letters, to and from. And a silly drawing Hamnet had made for him in honor of his birthday. All gone now, all ashes. The mere thought of beginning again had quenched his own fire. He could not let in happen again.

Will ransacked a stack of belongings in the corner to retrieve his spyglass, which he held up to a small chink—sweet, lovely chink!—in the shutters facing his neighbor's property.

"What can you see?" Xander wanted to know.

"Not much," Will grumbled. "A lot of yellow. Alvah's trees are far enough from his house that I think the woods will be fine if the house burns fast enough. It's the grass I'm worried about. That could bring the flames right to our palisade. We may have to go out and do what we can to divert it, monster or no."

Margaret spoke up, then. "Perhaps the fire has frightened the thing away."

"I'd hate to stake my life onperhaps, but we may have no choice." Turning to Xander, he added, "Once we're outside, I'll need you to fetch the spade. Margaret, you bring the bucket."

Xander threw up his arms in frustration. "How is that going to help?"

"You're going to dig up and throw dirt on any flaming grass you see near our wall."

When everyone was ready, Will led the way. "In fact, you can start on a rough trench now. Margaret, I know it's idiotic and very likely futile, but you'll need to fetch water from Xander's Run to douse the flames."

"And what are you going to do?" said Xander.

"Besides panic? I'll be covering the both of you with these guns. If we're lucky, some of the other neighbors have been watching this disaster unfold and have either gone to get help or are making bucket brigades of their own."

Once out-of-doors, Xander and Margaret rushed off about their tasks leaving Will alone with the night. Somewhere in the darkness, he knew, Grendel watched and waited, perhaps still gorging himself on members of Alvah's family. At least, Will hoped it to be so, for if it was, it meant the beast would not be coming for him and his anytime soon—a terrible, black wish, but there it was. It seemed ages before Xander returned with his spade—and an extra, for good measure.

Will pointed some fifteen to twenty feet ahead. "Scrape out a line there, as best you can, then go back and widen it. It needn't be deep, but wide." He waved his arm from east to west to illustrate how long the line should be.

At length, Will heard the sound of someone shuffling

towards him and looked to see Margaret struggling along with the rain barrel in her arms. He said nothing the while, not wanting to interrupt her concentration. At last, she reached his side and slowly squatted low enough to set the massive thing down with a dull, sloshing thud.

"Good god, woman! Even a horse doesn't weigh so much as that barrel!"

"Yes," she grunted, panting heavily.

"I asked only for a bucket."

Margaret shot him a grim look. "I am not going into the forest in the dark even once to fetch water."

Will reached up and put an arm 'round her shoulder. "With strength like yours, you've got nothing to fear."

Margaret took another moment to compose herself and then picked up the extra spade.

"No, no," said Will. "You've done enough. Here." He passed his pistol and musket over and took the shovel for himself. "I'll do this, and you can stand guard."

It was, of course, the chivalrous thing to do, but he regretted it within a couple of minutes' time, for his was not a young back, and his knees had not been kind to him for decades now. And his shoulder and forearm continued to complain. Still, if such action brought him closer to his son and to Margaret, it would be well worth the inevitable aches and pains that came later. If there was a later.

At some point, Margaret insisted on trading places with Will. He'd made tremendous progress, but in no wise could he keep pace with Xander. He protested Margaret's gesture half-heartedly, but knew she was right, and so returned to his station, holding both pistol and musket out into the dancing shadows of darkness and flame. By his best guess, the fire blazed for well over an hour, devouring the neighbor's home, until it found nothing left to sustain it. There being no wind, the flames had nowhere to go and thus slowly subsided. Xander and Margaret abandoned their task, too, seeing that their home and its demesnes appeared safe for the nonce.

"One of you should go and get some sleep," said Will. "The other can stay with me. In a few hours, you can switch places."

It was obvious that Margaret was not going to leave Will's side, and Xander was only too happy accept the suggestion. Once he had gone back to the cottage, Margaret said, "You're the one who should be sleeping right now. If we lose you..."

"You'll not lose me," Will countered. "I do believe all this activity and exercise have been good for me. I may lack your herculean strength, but I feel stronger than I have in years. The air in London is not 'o the best, as you know. And in Warwickshire, I had little to do but sit in my garden and drink all day."

"There was no monster in London," Margaret replied.

"Wasn't there?" said Will. "I can think of several—poverty, greed, indolence, o'er-weening ambition, corruption, syphilis, the plague..."

Never taking her eyes off the fire, Margaret said, "This one, though, this Grendel, must needs be dispatched as soon as possible. I would not die by his hands."

"If hands they are."

A voice sounded up the road. Neighbors come at last to investigate, to fight the flames, to see what might be done.

"Hello, the road!" Will called out.

"Hello!" several voices called back. So, not just one neighbor, but several.

Soon, a party of them came over a rise in the fields, bearing torches, tools and weapons. Naturally, they'd come to investigate the fire. But if they meant to kill William and Margaret...He lowered his musket and tucked his pistol into his belt. He could still get a shot off if needed. As the group drew nearer, Will struggled in the gloom to separate those faces he recognized from those he did not. From the corner of his eye, he noticed that Margaret still held her spade and, in fact, had lifted it into a self-protective position. He could not blame her.

One of the familiar faces stepped forward. "Well met, Master Kemp."

Well met? It was neither the time of day nor circumstances under which he'd say such a thing himself, but neither was it meet to quibble. "If you've come to put out yon fire, I'm afraid you're a bit late," he said.

The other man offered a grim snort in response. "I believe

you have the right of it. But we heard screams and cries and musket fire." He cast an accusatory eye at Will's weapons. "Belike you can tell us more?"

Will did not like the man's tone, but understood that failure to cooperate would look suspicious. "We heard the same. Roused us from bed, it did."

The neighbor drew closer. "You saw nothing, then?"

"Not until that fire had fairly engulfed the cottage."

"You saw no savages...?"

"It is well-known there's a horrible beast in these parts," Margaret cut in, apparently fed up with the stranger's roundabout manner. "Did you not hear its roar?"

"We heard it!" another man called from the back of the group. "We all heard it."

"And you think we made that roar?" Margaret pressed on.

"Well, no," the man said, "I was just being thorough..."

"You were just being officious," she snapped. "Master Kemp has asked for help in dealing with this creature countless times, only to be told that it's no immediate threat. What do you all say now?"

"We don't know," a third man said, "as it's your beast. Might 'ave been a bear."

Margaret shook her head in disgust. "The same old answer, too. A bear. Let us all go over there come sun up and see what your bear has done."

"I didn't say it was a bear," the man replied defensively. "Only as it might 'ave been."

A fourth man stepped forward, his wife at his side. "I for one would be happy to survey the scene with you in the morning. I'm Rogers, by the way. James Rogers, and this is my good wife, Emily."

"How do you do, mistress?" Will inquired of the woman.

"I wish I could say it was a pleasure, Master Kemp," she replied, nodding at the nearby destruction. "It is difficult to be hopeful in such circumstances."

"I cannot help but agree. Still, I will welcome you and your husband's company on the morrow, if we should happen to meet again."

"What will you do now?" Rogers asked.

"Barricade ourselves into our home 'til sunrise, I suspect. And you?"

"The lot of us is patrolling the area," the bear-man cut in.

"Excellent," said Will. "Then Margaret and I shall leave you to it."

"Every throng, it seems, contains mankind in miniature," Will observed once he and Margaret were safe inside their cottage. "There are the good, the bad, and those too busy trying to survive to decide which side they're on."

"That's most of us, I'll warrant."

"William..." Margaret was jostling him, gently. Time to wake. Will groaned and sat up. How was it possible he felt more tired after sleep than he had before? *This was sometimes a paradox, but now the time gave it proof.* "*You* haven't slept, though," he told his friend.

"I'll sleep in a few hours. After we've investigated the ruins of Alvah's home."

"Mmm. Xander up yet?"

"I'm up!" came the answer from the other room.

Giving his eyes a vigorous rub, Will got to his feet and hobbled into the main room, wherehe found bread, cheese and watery ale waiting for him. "Never been much of a water drinker, but it's so pure in Virginia, I think I prefer it to beer."

Margaret gasped in mock astonishment. "Perish the thought!"

Xander was busy adjusting his clothing, which was fast becoming too small for him. Seeing the boy's frustration, Will said, "We'll visit the tailor and buy you some new clothing. Mind you, it won't be so fashionable, but it should be a great deal more comfortable and appropriate for this New World."

"Today?" Xander asked hopefully.

"Today," Will confirmed. "I'm sure they'll have questions in town about last night's events and maybe, at long last, they'll be motivated to help find and kill our monster."

The room smelt of smoke—mere prologue, Will suspected,

to what they'd encounter out of doors. He retrieved his musket from the bench where Margaret had placed it and handed his pistol to Xander, whose face then shone with a radiance Will had never before seen.

"You're letting me carry this?" said Xander.

"And use it, too, if it comes to that," Will answered. "Think you can figure it out?"

"It's just point and shoot, isn't it?"

"Oh, aye, but she'll kick back on you. Hold your hand as firmly as you may." He winked at Margaret and she smiled in return, validating his decision to give Xander more responsibility.

In two short minutes, they were out into the August morning, which did indeed reek of smoke. Again, there was dew on the grass, which might have helped to explain why the previous night's fire hadn't spread towards their home. They walked past the barrel Margaret had set down, past the trench she and Xander had etched into the earth, and over the crest in their fields 'til they had a clear view of Alvah's property.

As expected, it was a blackened and still-smoking shell of its former self, a foreboding stain on the otherwise pristine landscape. A small crowd of folks had already gathered to walk the perimeter, though no one seemed eager to cross into the ashes proper. An odor reached Will's nostrils then, something between roast meat and a charnel house. Sadly, he'd smelled worse on other occasions, but he could see the stink didn't agree with either of his companions, and it was certainly something one never got used to.

"Foh!" Xander exclaimed. "Is that bodies?"

"Man and beast alike, I should think," Will answered. "We heard them all dying last night."

Closer still, they could feel the heat coming off the place where bright orange embers still smoldered.

"Master Kemp!" one of the onlookers called out as he waved to Will. It was young Rogers again and his charming wife. Will acknowledged the man's presence with a wave of his own and then returned his attention to the ruins.

"Probably best to keep black powder out of this mess," said he, as he handed his musket to Margaret. "I need to go into the yard and see what the dead have left to tell us."

Xander was about to ask if he might accompany his father when he caught Margaret's eye and she cut him off with a silent shake of her head. Too dangerous.

As Will ventured into the ashes, he felt as if he were walking on the surface of a barely frozen pond, or perhaps trying cross a creek by stepping on its most prominent stones. Every step was a trial and he feared the wrong verdict. The ground beneath his boots was still warm, but not alarmingly so. Nevertheless, he was not anxious to step into a hole that had been hidden by ash, stumble over an unseen rock, or land upon a still-blazing coal. He wished he'd thought to bring his cane with him, that he might move with greater confidence, but tumbling into the soot was the least of his worries, for he thought he spied the remains of Alvah's hog in the shadows ahead.

Strangely, he feared to approach it, and why should that be so? He'd seen dead and butchered animals—men, too—why should a slaughtered and incinerated hog bother him? Looking up, he observed that virtually everyone within eyesight was watching him, waiting for his next step, his next move, allowing him to be the sacrifice should anything go awry. A thousand clever quotes entered his mind then, but he dismissed 'em all. There was no poetry in this desolation, as there should not have been. With a sigh of resignation, he advanced on the pig's corpse. Ah. Partially buried beneath it was Alvah's body. Part of it, anyway. The geometry of the visible leg and lower torso would not accommodate an entire man. But that mystery could wait. Will bent down and studied the hog. Contrary to what Will might have expected, its throat was not slashed, its belly not ripped asunder. Instead, an enormous bite had been taken from the back of its neck and through the spine, so that only the flesh beneath its jaw still connected it to the body. There were great gouges in the animal's face, too, and along its sides, and one of its hind legs had been torn off. All of this, of course, had occurred before it had been burnt in the fire. This close, Will could not avoid the aroma of roast pork, commingled, he knew, with that of roast Alvah. Nevertheless, his stomach rumbled with hunger. What a piece of work is man, indeed.

"What do you see there, Master Kemp?" Someone called out.

"Alvah and his prize sow. Or parts of 'em, anyway." Will worked his way past fallen timbers towards the cottage door. Another body, this one missing an arm, lay halfway across the threshold. Like the others, it was thoroughly scorched, so that all its features had been erased. By its size, though, Will guessed it was one of the younger children. Around the yard and inside the cottage frame, there were other, similar lumps and mounds of his former neighbors and their pets. But there was nothing that corresponded to Alvah's wife or his eldest son. Retracing his steps, Will nearly tripped on Alvah's musket, half-sunken in blood-soaked soot. With great care, he lifted the thing from the mess and wiped it off as best he could. It had been fired, but he already knew that. What surprised him was that it was still operable.

"That his musket you've got there?" Another man yelled.

"That it is."

"May as well keep it. Bein' his nearest neighbor, you might need the extra firepower."

If the comment was meant to bolster Will's spirits, it had the opposite effect. He looked over at Margaret and Xander, who watched his every move with obvious trepidation. He offered a wan smile.

The closer he looked at things, the more evidence of violence he saw. And it was clear, incontrovertibly clear to him that it had not been perpetuated by the Powhatans, but instead, as he'd already divined, by Grendel. Satisfied that the site had nothing left to tell him, he turned and followed his own tracks out, which effort seemed to convince the gathering crowd that exploration was now safe for everyone. Within seconds, at least ten of his fellow settlers were combing through the ash and ruins for anything that might be salvaged, saved or traded. To Will's mind, it was grave robbery, and yet he would not part with Alvah's musket now that he'd seen up close what Grendel could do to a family.

"What do you make of it all?" Margaret asked.

"The beast killed 'em; of that I've no doubt. But how and

why the fire started I can only guess."

"Maybe they meant to frighten him away with a flaming brand or lantern, but dropped it by mistake," Xander said.

Will arched his eyebrows at the boy. "'Tis entirely plausible, perhaps even likely. But now, let's get Margaret home to bed, and you and I will venture into town."

~ 28 ~

IN THY ORISONS
BE ALL MY SINS REMEMBER'D

Jamestown, September, 1619

The walk into Jamestown seemed shorter than usual, though whether that was because Will's feet were unusually cooperative, because Xander was there for company (and still carried the flintlock), or because the trip had become routine, Will could not say, but he was more than glad of it. Of his own accord, Xander began to sing *The Three Ravens* and Will, in an especially good mood despite the previous night's horror, jumped in to harmonize as best he might.

> There were three ravens sat on a tree
> Down-a-down, Hey! Down-a-down,
> And they were black as they might be...

It was not a cheerful tune, nor a happy tale it told, but it lifted Will's spirits just the same. "You've an excellent voice, son," said he.

"The customers made me sing often, when they weren't... when they weren't..."

"Yes," Will cut in. "Well, you're well out of that now. You are your own master here, and no one can make you do anything against your will."

Xander giggled.

"What?" Will demanded.

"You said will."

"Yes, well it can hardly be avoided. And it is my name, after all."

"But it means…"

Will rolled his eyes and growled in playful exasperation. "I bloody well *know* what it means, lad." He cleared his throat. "Perpend:

Whoever hath her wish, thou hast thy Will,
And Will to boot, and Will in overplus;
More than enough am I that vex thee still,
To thy sweet will making addition thus.
Wilt thou, whose will is large and spacious,
Not once vouchsafe to hide my will in thine?
Shall will in others seem right gracious,
And in my will no fair acceptance shine?
The sea, all water, yet receives rain still,
And in abundance addeth to his store;
So thou being rich in Will add to thy Will
One will of mine, to make thy large Will more.
Let no unkind, no fair beseechers kill;
Think all but one, and me in that one Will."

Xander laughed so hard at this that he nearly dropped the pistol. "Will!" he cried joyfully. "Large and spacious! Oh, say it again! Say it again!"

Will turned to the trees on his left, breaking an invisible fourth wall with a small bow, and smirked, "I have found my true audience, at last." The trees did not laugh, but Xander continued to do so. Not wishing to dampen the boy's mood, Will recited the sonnet again. And again. At last, Xander's merriment subsided, as it must, and Will grew downright melancholy.

He'd never heard his natural son laugh so heartily and never would. Of all those he missed in his former life, it was Hamnet he missed the most—and he had been gone the longest. Clipped before his time, before he'd 'gun to bud. Not Hamlet, nor Lear, Othello or any of the others approached the tragedy of it. And therein had William failed. These plays were but the shadows of his sorrow.

Before they reached the village proper, they were met by a large group of men, including the governor, heading in the opposite direction.

"Good morrow, Master Kemp," Sir George called out.

"I was just coming to see you," Will said.

"I am certain you were, but I must see the damage for myself first."

"Of course."

A look of concern came over the governor's face just then as he considered Xander. "Do you mean to take your young apprentice here into the village?"

Will put a hand on Xander's arm to reassure the boy. "I do," said he.

"Hmmm," the governor grunted. "That may not be the best idea, under the circumstances."

"And what circumstances are those?" asked Will, taken aback.

The governor took a deep breath and let it out slowly. He turned to the rest of his entourage. "You men go ahead. I'll be along shortly."

Will felt the slow burn of building irritation coming on. "What's this about?"

The other man looked him dead in the eyes. "Might as well say it straight out: A ship came in a while back, an English ship flying Dutch flags. They traded a number of slaves—African slaves—for food, water and other supplies."

"Ah, yes. I'd forgotten," Will said, more to himself than anyone else. "But slaves..."

"Yes, and I thought, perhaps, your apprentice might find that...distressing."

"My apprentice might find that distressing? I fucking find it distressing. I was...I had a close relationship with an African woman once. I cannot imagine her doomed to a life of bitter durance and servitude."

For once, Sir George had no immediate response. After an uneasy pause that seemed to span the transition from summer to winter, he said, "Nonetheless, slaves there are in Jamestown now. The farmers swear by them. I expect there will be more soon." With that, he offered a polite nod and hurried up the trail after his men.

"African slaves?" Xander said.

"I'm afraid I've lost interest in going into the village today," Will confessed.

"But I've never seen an African."

"Nor a slave, I'll warrant." Will pulled his son closer. "Come, boy. Another time. We'll return home and ask Margaret to make us some honey cakes. How will that be?"

In a mere few months, some things, some behaviors and practices had already become routine in Will's new home. Evenings, for example, were now a time of boisterous songs, of overly dramatic readings, and of lewd poetry. Beer and wine flowed freely and tobacco and even cannabis were enjoyed by all. It was, to Will's mind, the Boar's Head made real and lacked only another voice or two to broaden the general antics. He supposed, in this scenario, that he was Sir John, which meant that Xander was Hal, and Margaret, Doll Tearsheet. But where was Poins? Where Pistol and Bardolph? He yearned, he realized, for his old, adoring audience. To recover them, though, was to uncover his duplicity and discover the life of pariah, for he had lied his way to this freedom he now enjoyed, and returning would likely do him more damage than good.

"Can you recite the work of any of your peers?" Margaret asked during a lull in the festivities.

"My peers? You wound me, woman, to suggest I have peers!"

"I do think, sirrah, that flattery's the last thing you need. But surely you know the works of Lily, of Spencer, of de Vere and others."

Will nearly choked on his ale. "De Vere?"

"Yes," said Margaret, alarmed by Will's reaction. "The late Earl of Oxford."

"I bloody well know he's the Earl of Oxford."

"Was," Xander added.

"Was," Will agreed. "I am very well acquainted with his so-called poems, for indeed I penned everything he ever wrote. Have you any idea how difficult it is to blunt your own genius, to subjugate it to another's narcissism?"

"Am I mad, or did you just claim you're the author of de Vere's poems?"

"Not only his poems, but diverse other of his writings, too—particularly his letters to Her Majesty. The Great Patron of the Arts could not tell a simile from a smile, an allusion from an illusion, or alliteration from alteration. A beadle's hangnail has more sense. Polyphemus had better vision! Indeed, the only talent old Ned ever possessed was that of profligate spendthrift. He even had the temerity to ask me for a loan once, whereof I learned the wisdom of "Neither a borrower nor a lender be." Born into a fortune, constantly gifted with more and more money by the crown and others, and yet, at the end, he'd very little to show for it. I, on the other hand, have…"

Will noticed his great speech had become a soliloquy, for Margaret and Xander had commenced to play cards, in apparent mockery of his boasting. He cleared his throat and stared at Margaret, who struggled to keep a straight face under such scrutiny. In a second, she was howling with laughter, only to be joined by Xander almost immediately and, inevitably, Will himself. Even Sir Doggles barked along from his place on the reed mat.

When Will paused to take another prodigious gulp of beer, Margaret changed the subject. "I understand," said she, "that you've grown tired of writing entire plays. But sonnets? Surely they don't require much effort."

"It isn't the effort. It is more that I've done about all I can do with blank verse. It has become too confining, like a coffin. And too predictable, like death. And I find I yearn for other rhythms now."

"Like?" Xander asked.

Will thought for a moment and then said, "Improbable dichotomy."

"Improbable dichotomy?" Margaret echoed.

"Diaphanous prolixity," Will added.

"Inedible felicity," said Margaret.

"Rhinoceros hypocrisy." Xander chimed in.

"Improbable dichotomy

Diaphanous prolixity
Inedible felicity
Rhinoceros hypocrisy!" Will sang out triumphantly.

"Yes," said Margaret, "I hear it. But what does it mean? It's all just nonsense, isn't it?"

Will made a face. "Must everything have meaning? Does *life*? What's wrong with enjoying something solely for its musicality?"

"Sounds a bit like ritual chanting or some such," Margaret said, "but I suppose if you like it, there's no reason you can't write in that meter. But what about your *Don Quixote*? Weren't you going to write something in that style?"

"I am hoping things will quiet down 'round here come wintertime. At present, it's rather difficult to concentrate with ruffians tormenting us, monsters devouring our neighbors and Lord knows what all else going on."

"Then," Margaret said, "we must do something about these ruffians and this monster ourselves."

Will offered a sinister laugh. "I was thinking," said he, "of introducing them to each other..."

If he could have bottled the looks of astonishment on Margaret's and Xander's faces, he might have sold the same at any market in Arabia.

"What do you mean?" Xander managed at last.

"Have you ever wanted to be in a play?" Will asked the boy.

~ 29 ~

SERVICE IS NO HERITAGE

Jamestown, September, 1619

The following day, Will decided to attempt Jamestown again, this time with Margaret at his side instead of Xander. They would see for themselves how and where theseslaves were employed, and to what extent, before determiningwhether the young man might in any way be distressed by this new development. Though the nights had gotten cooler of late, the days continued to bake the fields and forests, turning the grass into so much straw and robbing the leaves of their luster. In the heat, the aroma of dust, of sap and sun-soaked stone predominated. It would not be too many weeks now, Will knew, before those leaves began to fall, changing the look of every horizon.

There was a crew at Alvah's place, and though Will only saw them from a distance, he suspected they were burying the dead—man and animal alike—and making sure that every last ember was extinguished. Perhaps he was meant to help in this endeavor, but the people of Jamestown had ignored his warnings about Grendel for so long that he felt resentful, as if Alvah's catastrophe was a direct result of the town's inaction. Still, he felt the acrid bite of indecision and almost retraced his steps, until Margaret propelled him forward.

"What's done cannot be now amended," she said.

"What's that from?"

Margaret stared at him, mouth agape. "You don't remember? *You?*"

"Ah," said Will. "One of mine, then. No, I don't remember every line of every play. Do you recall every line you've ever memorized?"

Margaret laughed. "I take your point." They walked a while in silence and then she said, "Your wife...what sort of woman is she?"

Will put his head down, as if he'd been expecting and dreading the question. "She's a fine woman, if I'm honest. Strong, good and true. I have contrived a galaxy of excuses for my actions, for my leaving her, but they are dark stars, these reasons, shedding no heat or light, and therefore doing no one any good. I feel no little shame at this, and yet, I could not endure the boredom or the claustrophobia of our marriage. Once, I'd have said 'Were man but constant, he were perfect.' Now? I am not so sure."

"And she thinks you dead, so you cannot make amends."

"By design. I must live with my choices."

"And so must she."

The comment stung. "I hope," said Will, "that with her newfound freedom and the money I've left her, she will not long mourn my absence. Perhaps she'll find cheer in her grandchildren."

"And our boy's mother? What can you share of her?"

"The wife I should have had, would have had, and I'd been worthy of her."

"Ah…" Margaret trailed off. "*If hairs be wires, black wires grow on her head.*"

Once more, Will was amazed, astounded at his companion's keen perception. "Yes. We used to stroll proudly, Luce and I, provocatively along the Thames of a Sunday, whilst all the zealots were in church."

"She was not a church-goer, either?"

A sad smile came to Will's lips then. "She was not welcome, of course. She always claimed it was due to her 'Luce morals,' but the truth is that they wouldn't allow her through the doors."

"When did you drift apart?"

Will shook his head, as if to banish the coming memories. "One of her other suitors made her a better offer, one I failed to counter."

Desperate to abandon the topic of his failings, Will asked, "And what of your past? You've never explained why you chose to come hither, trading the comforts of London for the dangers of the New World."

Margaret extended a hand and swept a low-hanging branch from her path. "I beat the wrong someone rather badly."

Will let that sit for a good, long while. "A brief loss of temper?"

"Not at all. Bastard had it coming."

"Well, I'm glad you didn't do it for your own amusement."

"Oh," said Margaret, "it was thoroughly enjoyable. I'm only sorry he didn't have brothers; then, I could have beaten them all."

"Bad sort, was he?"

"The worst."

"And, er, he tried to assault you, perhaps?"

"Close" Margaret admitted. "He assaulted my companion, another one...like me...only much smaller."

"Margaret, my friend, Prometheus was smaller than you."

She gave him a playful shove that almost sent him head-first into the nettles by the side of the road. "Anyway, there are those who sate their lust upon us, who, once finished, are overtaken by a strange self-loathing, and since they're too cowardly to punish themselves—if punishment were even necessary—they take it out on us. This one broke Bet's arm, and in return I broke his knave's pate."

Will nodded. It seemed an entirely reasonable response to him. "And were you often subject to such violence?"

"Not often, no. But there have always been those who hate us for existing, or themselves for wishing to be like us. It gets awfully tedious after a time, I must say."

"And now?"

"I thought that I could hide from such people, but I see they exist wherever men exist. I have suffered the cold stares in town, and shall again today, I have no doubt. But I have found you and Xander, and never have I felt more at home." So saying, she leaned Will's way and planted a kiss ever-so-lightly upon his left cheek.

"I am glad of it," Will winked.

As they emerged from the forested part of their journey and into the fields surrounding Jamestown, they saw that, yes, there were Africans working in the tobacco fields.

"And these are their lives, now?" Will asked quietly. "Whatever dreams, whatever aspirations they may have had are now erased forever? My gorge rises at it."

"And might not the same happen to Xander, to me, to anyone? This frights me more than Grendel."

"Indeed: bondage or death?"

Margaret pulled him closer, and the pair finished their walk into town in troubled silence. They purchased fresh supplies and foodstuffs, a serviceable change of clothing for Xander, and made their way back home as quickly as possible.

And Summer's Lease Hath All Too Short a Date

Except, it seemed, in Virginia, where the oppressive heat continued well into September. In attempt to keep cool, Will agreed to wander over to Xander's run with the boy and Sir Doggles. What he daren't admit was that he was afraid to let his son wander alone. Again. He might drown, after all. He might fall. Xander was slightly older, yes, and more self-aware in some ways than Hamnet; still, Will did not believe he could survive another son's loss.

Now, as restorative as the creek's cool waters were, the antics of his son and dog were even more so, chasing one another, chasing crayfish, chasing the sun as it sparkled across the ripples and eddies, chasing the waning moments of summer. Will passed the time sitting on a shady stretch of the near bank, dangling his feet in the water and trying his best not to let his mind wander either forwards or backwards. Here, now, he was happy.

After a while, both boy and dog plopped themselves down at Will's side, to rest and recuperate before resuming their joyful romp. It ought to have been a beautiful moment.

Instead, it shattered Will's world.

How many times he'd seen the boy's feet, he couldn't begin

to guess. He'd never truly looked at them, though. Or maybe he had and simply refused to register what he now saw too plainly: the second and third toes on Xander's left foot were webbed together at the first joint. And Will's toes were not, no, but he knew someone else with the very same trait. Yes, he did. His friend Richard Burbage had identical webbing on his corresponding toes.

Xander was not Will's boy, but Richard's.

Hence, the boy's given name.

Thou shouldst not have been old till thou hadst been wise.

Abruptly, Will felt like a wineskin that had sprung a leak, his substance, his vigor, his purpose slowly draining from him. He hung his head as he grappled with a wave of melancholy and then outright despair.

"Are you ill, father?" Xander asked, suddenly aware of Will's change in demeanor.

"No, no," Will answered. "It is nothing. A slight pain behind my eyes. That is all." But it was not all. The boy was not his son, natural or otherwise. Will felt the loss almost as acutely as he'd felt Hamnet's, for it was a second death of hope, and what then was the point in anything?

"I'm hungry," Xander exclaimed. "Shall I go and see if supper is ready?"

Will nodded. "Aye, do boy, do." And once Xander and his dog were out of sight and hearing, Will wept. It began slowly enough, but soon became a torrent, a tempest of grief, of shame, of self-pity and more. He wept for all he'd lost and for all he'd thrown away. And then, of course, he felt ashamed.

But, you must know, your father lost a father;
That father lost, lost his, and the survivor bound
In filial obligation for some term
To do obsequious sorrow...

And so it was for fathers mourning sons.

Still, Xander was *alive*, and son or no, he clept William father, and father he would be. And why not? He had loved Richard, he had loved Luce, and he knew now that he loved their son. His son, for Luce had deemed it should be so.

And then there was Margaret, who, in a few short months had grappled herself to his soul with hoops of steel. He could not imagine a future without her and promised himself he would never experience such a thing.

Will rose from the creek bank, fully aware of both the man he'd been and the opportunity ahead of him. By the time he reached the cottage, he was as light of heart, as buoyant, as a newlywed, which only made Margaret skeptical.

"Why do you smile so, old man?" she teased.

"Do not my smiles become me well?" Will laughed.

"Much better than your frowns. But what's the occasion?"

"Must there be an occasion? I'd as lief demand the sun wherefore he shines."

"And therefore, you are like the sun?"

"Like the son? I *love* the son!"

Confused by his spontaneous jollity, Margaret said, "Tis lack of food makes you play the fool. Come in, sir, come in and dine."

"Will!" Margaret hissed in his ear. "Will, wake up!"

"Yes Anne, yes, yes."

"William Kemp!"

He opened his eyes to his darkened bedroom, his thoughts still muddled from sleep. "What is it?" he whispered at Margaret, whose eyes were as wide as saucers.

"Listen."

He did so, hearing nothing at first, and then, somewhere off in the night came the anguished cry of a woman in torment, in utter and abject despair. Will sat up, held his breath. The cry faded into silence. Moments later, it sounded again, weaker or farther off. And then—oh, horror!—a baby's wail, travelling past Will's home at the speed of a horse's gallop, from faint to blaring and back to faint. Just when it seemed that silence had returned for good, a dreadful and dreadfully familiar howling roar reverberated through the night. A last, final cry from the child's mother (or so Will supposed her to be), and then all was quiet.

There would be no more sleeping this night.

"If Sir George doesn't send every man in the colony after this beast in the morning, there's no hope for the fellow," Will remarked.

The governor did send out another hunting party, but it fell far, far short of Will's expectations and, predictably, no beast was found, which only served to infuriate and motivate Will all the more to seek justice himself.

~ 30 ~

I'll Make Assurance Double Sure

Jamestown, October, 1619

One afternoon, the work crew sent one of its members through the palisade to knock upon the cottage door and inform Will that they would, at long last, be finished with the job the following day and expected payment at that time.

"And payment you shall have," Will responded in his best Titus Andronicus, to the complete befuddlement of the other man.

At the close of work the next day, Will came outside and laid a sheet of vellum on the stump normally used for splitting firewood, and set a shallow dish of ink beside it.

"What's this, then?" one of the workers demanded, sharing a look of great suspicion with his fellows.

"A contract. You're simply going to provide a thumbprint to indicate that you've completed the work as requested."

"What?" said another. "Ain't it customary to use a quill for this? To make an x, like?"

"You are absolutely right," Will said. "Alas, I am fresh out of suitable feathers. But this should serve just as well."

The first man who'd spoken, a large, stocky character, answered, "It's all one to me, long as I get my pay."

The rest of his crew muttered, mumbled and grumbled but soon agreed. One by one, they stepped up to the stump, dipped their thumbs into the ink, blotted them on the wood, and pressed them onto the parchment, whereupon Will placed the agreed-upon sum into their hands.

The man who'd been avoiding Will made a point of turning to him after receiving his money and said, "Pleasure doing business with you, sir."

"I couldn't agree more!" Will replied. "And, in truth, I may have other tasks for you all if you're interested."

"I never object to more coin," said a third, heretofore silent fellow.

Will offered a hearty laugh—the same he'd used in countless other performances. "You're a wise man, sir. And I shall look for you in town as soon as I determine my next project."

But he could hardly wait to get back inside once the men had gone. He rushed to his table and fetched both a candle and the glass he used for magnification. Next, he brought forth the sketch of the thumbprint he'd drawn some weeks earlier and set it next to the contract. "Come," he urged Margaret, "help me look at these prints for a match."

Xander, who'd been dozing in the loft, climbed down the ladder and joined them.

They weren't at it long, before Margaret cried out, "There!"

Will, whose eyesight was not quite so strong, leaned closer to the thumbprint in question, so that the tip of his nose almost rubbed against it. "I believe you're right."

"Let me see!" Xander insisted. After a moment's perusal, he concurred.

"But how do we know which man made which print?" Margaret asked.

Will stood up to his full height and stretched a kink out of his back. "I may lack your skills in the kitchen, milady, but I can remember faces like Da Vinci. I know who made each of those prints."

"Then we have our culprit?"

"One of them, anyway. Now, we must make him speak."

"What are we doing out here?" Xander asked his father, scanning the tall grass and the tree line for threats.

"I need your help," Will said.

"So you said, but what are we doing?"

Will handed the boy a spade. "We're going to move that rock, I hope, and then you are going to do a little digging."

"For?"

"A package of sorts."

"Which you put here, I'm guessing?"

"Er, yes."

"Why?"

"You shall see, anon. Let's move this stone."

"If you buried whatever-this-is by yourself last time, why do you need my help in digging it up now?" Xander demanded.

"Because I cherish your company," Will answered with equal parts sarcasm and sincerity.

The boy snorted and bent to help move the stone. That done, Will handed him a spade. "And now I get to dig?"

"'Tis a most useful skill, lad. Gravediggers are never without work."

Xander cast him a worried look. "I'm not digging a grave, though, am I?"

"Only the means to fill one."

Xander sighed, stood, and leaned upon the spade. "You may be a poet, but I am not. What are you saying? What is this all about?"

Will pointed to the spot where the stone had been. "In the earth, there, you'll find a bundle that offers the means to rid ourselves of our enemies forever."

"Poison? Why d'you keep it way out here?"

"They love not poison that do poison need."

Xander began to dig. "And who are we poisoning?"

"That is the question! One man, I am sure of. And we shall use him to identify the rest."

"But..." Xander hesitated, "what about the bodies?"

"We're only in act three, my lad. Let me worry about act five."

The boy shrugged and resumed his digging. Eventually, he hit upon and uncovered the bundle Will had placed there months earlier. "Now what?"

"If you wrong us, shall we not revenge?"

Back in the cottage, Will put a small quantity of wine into a pot and placed it over the fire. Into this, he sprinkled mulling spices.

Margaret and Xander watched with great curiosity. Once the wine was simmering, Will added a third of his remaining opium—a frighteningly large amount—and mixed it into the wine. While this cooked, he retrieved his most ornate, most beautiful bottle and set it onto the table. Next, he fetched the funnel he used for his alchemical experiments and also a full bottle of wine. Then, he returned to the wine on the fire. "Double double, toil and trouble, fire burn and cauldron bubble," he cackled.

"Have you ever killed a man before?" Margaret cut in.

"In war."

"This isn't war."

"Isn't it?" Will countered.

"And you tell me to screw my courage to the sticking place, I'll know you've gone mad."

Will turned to regard his friend, delight evident in his gaze. "You are a rare one. I do not doubt your acting company has perished in your absence."

"And you," Margaret said, "are being evasive."

"Very well," said Will, rubbing his hands together, as if to remove the residue of opium, "these men have beaten you almost to death, nearly murdered me, and continue to pester and plague us. The governor has not exposed or punished them, and it is clear he never will."

"But if you're found out..."

Will took the mulled wine off the fire and set it on a board atop the table, where it scorched the wood, smoldered and steamed. "Such a tyrant, that little 'if.' I stand amazed at all that might have been but for his censure, and that of his brother, 'no.' But I shall not be discovered; you have my word."

"Let's assume you are correct. How are you planning to use this potion of yours?"

"I know the face of the man who threw stones at our home. I have but to go into town, find him, and invite him here, under the pretext of hiring him for more work. He will drink some wine, and then I shall extract some answers from him."

"Unless he is asleep," Margaret said dryly.

Again, Will offered his malevolent cackle. "Oh, I think he'll find that difficult."

~ 31 ~

WHY THEN TONIGHT
LET US ASSAY OUR PLOT

Jamestown, October, 1619

It was a while before Will located the man in question—a squinty-eyed fellow with an oft-broken nose—and begged him to come visit to discuss building a smokehouse before the winter frost came.

The man haggled, of course, but as he'd never see a penny of the agreed-upon price, Will was content to let him win. And it was another week before the man arrived at the cottage to discuss the job. By prior agreement, both Margaret and Xander were out of the cottage. Will would not have them tainted by what was to come.

The villain swaggered into Will's home as if he lived there himself. "Where are your friends?" he sneered.

"Gathering nuts in the forest, as I understand. They should return at any time."

The other man nodded and looked about himself, clearly searching out objects of value for later theft. "Right," said he. "So, about this job, then."

"Yes, yes," said Will. "But first, a glass of wine. I'm sure you're thirsty from the walk." Will gestured to the ornate bottle on the table.

His guest could not keep the avarice from his eyes. "I won't say no," the man confessed.

"I am already halfway through my second cup, but I'll pour one for you."

Oh, but the fellow was eager. Was he a drunkard, or merely anxious to taste what he thought was a more-expensive wine than he'd ever before sampled? It hardly mattered. It was the last wine he'd ever taste. Will handed him the cup and then lifted his own untainted wine to his lips. The man took a large sip and then said, "Spiced, is it?"

"In accordance with the season," Will replied. "Is it too much?"

"No, sir. Just...unusual is all." Not unusual enough, however, to preclude a second sip and a third. By the time the man had gotten halfway through his cup, he began to slow down. "Mind if I sit?" he asked and sat without waiting for an answer. "This is strong stuff you gentlemen drink."

Within a few minutes, he was slumping in his chair, struggling to stay upright. Confused, but not angry. Will reached across the table and jabbed a finger into the man's chest and was rewarded with an idiotic smile but no resistance.

"I do believe it is time to restrain you," Will said, producing a small loop of leather cordage from his waistcoat. In short order, he had the man's ankles and wrists tied to the chair. "Comfortable?" he asked.

"Mmmmnnn," said his guest.

"You attacked my friend Margaret, did you not?"

"S' what if I did?"

"Did'st think I'd deliberate forever, villain?" Will breathed. "Though the day be long, yet midnight comes at last. Who else was involved?"

The man's head lolled to-and-fro, but he remained quiet.

Will stabbed him in the left shoulder with a small knife, eliciting no response. "Interesting." He held the candle flame to the man's left ear.

"Stop. Stop," the man moaned lazily, as if he weren't fully invested in the matter. "Sanders, Birch, Whitfield and..."

"And?"

"Did I say 'Dagget'?"

"You did not."

"Dagget."

"You're from Newgate, you lot, yes?"

"Mmmm," the fellow intoned. "Did I say 'Sanders'?"

Will held the man's cup to his lips. "Drink up, friend."

In the end, Will had to force a half bottle down the man's throat before he died.

Later, when Margaret and Xander returned, Margaret carried the shroud-wrapped corpse off into the woods and down to the James by a roundabout path, careful to avoid being seen. Once she achieved the shore, she placed several stones inside the shroud and dragged the body out into the river, almost up to her chin. Will had been very specific in his instructions that he wanted the body heavy enough to avoid the river's surface, but not so much that it wouldn't tumble along with the current. With any luck their dead friend would find the sea in three or four days, never to be seen again.

While she was about her business, Xander sat silently by the fire, brooding.

"It had to be done," Will explained. "If we're to catch the rest of our tormentors."

Xander said nothing.

"It doesn't mean that I…"

"What?" the boy said, "You think I've never killed anyone?"

Will felt as if he'd been poleaxed. "Why then, we've all killed someone," he declared with a sheepish grin.

"Margaret, too?" Xander asked with increasing irritability.

Recognizing that he'd gone too far, Will said, "I was attempting a little humor. That is all. But I am sorry to have distressed you so."

"I am not distressed. I just hoped I had escaped such things in leaving London."

Slowly, quietly, Will sat on the floor beside his son and joined him in staring into the fire.

"I killed my first man when I was ten," Xander said quietly. "In revenge for…in revenge. There's a lot of bad happens to a boy in a whorehouse." Will knew better than to speak at this moment. "And it was hurt this man, or…anyway, I had no choice. A couple of years later, this one bastard was beating one of the girls something awful. None of the other girls could get him off her, get him to stop. So, I stopped him with a kitchen knife."

"I hope she'll forgive me for telling you, but you and Margaret share a similar experience, though I don't think her man died."

Finally, Xander looked over at Will. "Is that true?"

Will nodded.

~ 32 ~

ALL THINGS ARE READY
IF OUR MIND BE SO

Jamestown, October, 1619

Another week or ten days passed before a group of citizens came by with a search party, scouring the area for any sign of the dead man. It was a larger party than Sir George had sent after the missing baby, which angered Will no end. Having spent most of his adult life in the theater, he had no difficulty feigning a most credible ignorance as to the dead man's whereabouts. *False face must hide what false heart doth know.* Fortuitously, two of the villains the dead man had named were in this group, which helped advance Will's plan to its next step.

"I have work for four or five men!" he said to the tallest of the group. "Come by at your convenience and I shall tell you the details, if gold dislike you not."

The men laughed, and the tall one said, "Tomorrow, then."

Tomorrow and tomorrow and tomorrow.

Sleep did not come easily to anyone in the cottage that night, and Will viewed it as a trade, an exchange: their own for the coming eternal sleep of his enemies.

When the men came by, they entered his home with the same swagger, the same arrogance their now-dead colleague had shown, as if they owned the place and everything in it—or would, eventually. Margaret waited in the bedroom with the musket, whilst Xander sat upon a stool in the corner, pretending to work with a piece of leather. Will placed a hand atop his own head—a signal to Xander that their performance was about to begin.

"Would anyone care for a cup of wine?" he asked the ruffians.

"Oh, aye!" one of them exclaimed.

Xander rose and moved to pour from Will's ornate bottle, when Will stopped him. "Not that one, boy," said he. "That's too dear for workaday drink! Fetch another."

"And why not that one?" one of the others asked.

"Oh," said Will, "that's likely the most expensive bottle of wine i' the New World. A renowned and powerful vintage. I'm saving it for a most special occasion."

Xander brought forth another bottle and poured a round for everyone save himself. The ruffians did not complain; second-best it may be, but it was still superior to anything they could purchase in town.

Will got down to business, telling his visitors he wished to have a smokehouse constructed, where, how large and other suchlike details. The tallest of the crew offered a price for the labor, Will haggled, and finally they reached an agreement.

"When can you start?" Will asked.

The tall man consulted his fellow and then answered, "This Wednesday, the 23rd."

"That's the full moon," Xander observed.

Tall man scowled at him contemptuously. "We won't be workin' that late, will we?"

Or breathing, thought Will. "Excellent," said he. "My companions and I are typically on our evening stroll in the hour or two before sunset, so don't be alarmed if you come knocking and we don't respond. We're always back well before dark."

The next morning, Will, Xander and Sir Doggles visited every neighbor within an hour's walk, which naturally took most of the day. Will wanted to buy some livestock—goat, sheep or pig-sized, but nothing so big as a cow. In the end, he was able to purchase three goats, from two different families. He told their initial owners that he wanted their milk and meat, come winter. But his actual plans were much darker.

"What shall we name them?" Xander asked, as he pulled them along behind him by three lengths of rope.

"Naming them is perhaps unwise," Will said, "given they won't be part of the family for long."

"Oh," said Xander, growing somber.

They tied their new animals to the fence surrounding the vegetable patch. There wasn't much left in the soil of interest to humans at this time of year, though the goats found plenty to eat. Sir Doggles was reluctant leave his caprine friends, but the hour approached for the family's new evening walks, and Will would not leave home without him. Before venturing outside the palisades, however, he made sure the stage was set inside the cottage. He'd hidden his books, verified that his ornate bottle of wine was in full view of the door, and even left some coin lying on a shelf near the cups, reasoning that if he was careless enough to leave wealth in plain view, he was too confident to hide anything of value. At least, that was the message he hoped to convey to the workers if they came by.

Everywhere one looked, trees blazed with autumnal fire in yellows, oranges and reds, which, though beautiful, did not warm Will's soul, for there was too much in the offing, too much on his mind to allow for present mirth. Nor was he alone in his preoccupation.

"When will they come by?" Xander asked out of nowhere.

"The rain cares nothing for the farmer's needs, but comes when it will, how it will. And so it is with prey and traps."

"Sometime over these next few days," Margaret added for clarification.

"I hate waiting."

"'Tis the affliction of the young."

Xander frowned. "And what is the affliction of the old?"

"That's a long list, lad, and I start it, I'll ne'er be done by the time our villains return."

"Then you recommend I not grow old?"

A look of sadness crossed Will's face so quickly that it might have been the shadow of a bird flying overhead. "Quite the contrary. I wish you a happy and lengthy life. Live your full measure, and cheat death every way you can. He's a greedy bastard, after all, and could use a little humbling."

When Will judged they'd been gone long enough, they returned to the cottage to find that nothing had changed. Though Xander and Margaret were disappointed not to have the whole thing over at last, Will took a more philosophical stance, seeing there were other things to be done that might increase the probability of his plan's success.

And the first of those was luring Grendel hither.

"Margaret," he said, as they settled into their evening routine, "I need your help outside a moment, before it gets well and truly dark."

"Whatever it is, I can do it!" Xander declared.

Will exchanged glances with Margaret, shrugged, and then said, "As you wish, young sir," whereupon he led Xander back outside and over towards the new livestock. "Choose one of them and bring him along. We're going outside the palisade for a moment."

Xander began to question his father, but thought better of it and did as he'd been told.

While he waited, Will looked up at his own tree in the gathering gloom. It did not blaze like the others they'd seen earlier. This tree bled, its leaves the color of old, dried blood, as they rustled to the ground like the cast-off scabs of a leper. The sight of them evoked only suffering and death.

And death was coming.

Having frightened himself almost into retreat, Will looked to the sky to steel himself, where a waxing gibbous moon stared back at him like an accusing eye.

"No help there," he muttered to himself as Xander approached. "Now," he said to the boy, "we are going through the gate, to tie our friend here to the other side of the wall."

Xander could hold his peace no longer. "But won't he get eaten by wild animals?"

"I am counting on it."

The young man balked, as if he might take the goat back to its fellows.

"Would you prefer to go back into the cottage?"

"Is there no there no other way?" Xander asked.

"None as likely to succeed, I think."

Xander nodded but remained silent.

Will unbarred the gate and led Xander and the goat through. "Tie it off there," he pointed to a particular spot on the wall. While the boy worked, Will drew his pistol and studied the surrounding fields. When Xander was done, he stepped back inside the palisade and began walking a back towards the cottage. Quickly, Will drew his dagger and made a long, shallow cut along the goat's left flank, much to the beast's dismay.

"What happened?" Xander called from the cottage door.

"Nothing of consequence," Will replied, as he ducked back inside the palisade himself and barred the gate, rattling it once or twice for good measure. The goat's bleating accompanied him all the way back to Xander's side.

"I don't understand."

"But you will, in time, and that is more than can be said of many a man."

A terrible, animal scream ripped through the night and hauled Will, Margaret and Xander from their beds. Sir Doggles barked as though pursued by the Devil himself.

The bait had been taken.

Xander came into the bedroom with the dog at his side to confirm the others had heard it, too, and seemed to breathe a sigh of relief to find them likewise awake and wary.

Will put out a hand, and Xander helped him rise to his feet, whereupon the older man made a circuit, again, of the cottage's shuttered windows and doors, and checked and rechecked that his pistol and the two muskets were loaded and ready to be fired if necessary. He placed another log on the fire as well, and stoked the embers beneath it.

"If our villains don't come tomorrow, we'll place a second goat outside the palisade by sundown."

"How if they come not before we've used all our goats?" Margaret asked.

"I shall try to purchase more—at greater cost, I shouldn't wonder."

"And then?"

"We shall learn which is the more seductive sin: our villains' greed or Grendel's gluttony."

As it turned out, the one fed the other.

~ 33 ~

NO BEAST SO FIERCE

Jamestown, October, 1619

It was Wednesday, October 23rd. The forest surrounding the Jamieson homestead was as still, as secretive as a graveyard, and the trees, stretching their increasingly skeletal branches towards the sky, seemed to be holding their collective breath in anticipation of…something momentous, something perhaps dire. There was a chill in the air, too, that discomforted not merely the skin, but the soul as well somehow, so that Will and his companions would like to have cut short their walk, but that their potential burglars needed time to enter their home—if they were entering today. Will glanced about at the drifts of dead leaves piled high against the undergrowth, almost like shrouds half-covering the dead. And there would be dead, he was confident. The only question was whether his enemies would die or he and his in attempting to trap them.

Though the sun had not entirely set, the full moon was rising over the roof of the cottage as the little family and dog returned from their walk. Upon seeing the front door slightly ajar, Will held out an arm to prevent his companions from proceeding into the house. He then passed his pistol to Xander, readied a musket and offered the second to Margaret, all without saying a word. He pointed to the Sir Doggles, whom Xander grasped by the collar and pulled close. Good, Will nodded. And then, as if his movements were somehow tied to the setting sun and rising moon, Will crept across the yard and towards the door. When he judged himself near enough, he stopped to listen. Hearing nothing, he advanced again. And stopped again. In time, he stood just outside the door proper, where he remained for the longest time, listening, waiting, and listening some more. The odors of wine and of sweat came to him then, and still he heard no sound from within. Stepping backwards, he nudged the door all the way open and thrust his musket into the opening.

There were bodies on the floor.

Without looking back, he waved for Margaret and Xander to join him. Once they reached his side, he whispered. "I'm going in. Shoot anything that moves on me."

Gloom had settled inside the cottage, seeming to grow darker by the second, and allowing the shadows to usurp the spaces normally owned by sun or flame or candlelight. Crossing to the fire, Will lit a taper and, with that, commenced to light every candle in the room. The time and space between each seemed to stretch into infinity, but at last he was done and could clearly see the figures laid out across his floor. There were three men, not four as he'd expected. Three, and all of them still breathed.

"We're missing one," Margaret said. The sudden eruption of her voice into the silence caught Will unprepared, and he nearly shrieked like a small child. In other circumstances, she would have laughed. Instead, she poked at one of the men with her musket. As he did not react, Will bent down and shook one of the others. The man made a sound somewhere between a giggle and a mumble and fell silent, whereupon Will got back to his feet.

"Margaret, love," he called softly, "do you recognize any of these men from the assault."

"All three," she answered grimly.

"You are certain?"

"Dead certain."

"Now's the time to step away if you don't wish to be involved. I can do this on my own," he said to Margaret and Xander.

"Go to!" Margaret responded. "I've as much a grudge against them as you, and I'll see them done for it."

Will turned to Xander. "I'd rather you stayed out of this part. This was my plan, and I'll take the consequences, whate'er they be. But I will not have you suffer for my choices."

Xander said nothing, but Will took his silence for agreement. Whether he agreed or no, Will would not have what was to come on the boy's conscience. "Would you fix a meal while Margaret and I finish this task?"

Xander passed the pistol back to Will, who shoved it into his belt and stooped low to grab one of the men by the arms. Without needing to be told, Margaret took hold of the man's ankles, and between the two of them, they dragged the fellow out the door. This action they repeated until they had removed all three men from their home. Next, they lugged each of them outside the palisade. It had gotten dark by this point, despite the full moon, and Will was loath to let Margaret return to the cottage for rope, but rope he needed and rope she retrieved. While she was gone, Will sat the men up against the palisade wall in the same spot where the first goat had been devoured, the stench of its viscera still permeating the area. Again, Margaret startled him, and again she did not laugh at him. This time, she understood the source of his fear and felt it herself. Working quickly, they tied up the would-be burglars and made certain they could neither rise nor escape the wall at their backs. Not that a single one of them was conscious enough to achieve such a feat, nor even to resist when Will carved a line across each of their faces. Immediately, they began to bleed and bleed profusely, and yet it didn't seem to bother them in the least. "Whether we fall by ambition, blood, or lust, like diamonds, we are cut with our own dust," he murmured to the last of them.

"Let us retreat while we may." Will said quietly.

Margaret fairly dragged him back inside the palisade and, from thence, into the cottage. With everything safely barred, bolted and locked behind him, Will exhaled mightily and threw himself down in his chair. Margaret picked up the ornate bottle, which she'd found on its side in the corner, and searched the floor for any other sign of the villains' presence in her home.

"I already picked up their cups," Xander offered.

"Good lad," Will said, tearing into a loaf of bread the boy had set out earlier.

Margaret and Xander joined him at the table, eating and

drinking in pensive silence. No one sang, nobody told any jokes, the lute stayed in its place on the shelf. The fire spoke merrily enough, but fires are always happy when they're eating. The family stubbornly kept its vigil in relative silence. As time wore on, however, Xander and Will nodded off to sleep—Xander, with his head down on the table, next to the still-unopened globe, and Will, sunken into his chair, snoring with a volume and ferocity that even the monster, Grendel, could not match.

Margaret jostled him awake, and, at first, Will didn't know where he was. Back in the ship's hold, crossing the Atlantic? Backstage at the Globe? In the attic of New Place, plotting his escape? When he saw the fear in Margaret's eyes, it all came back to him. He looked about the room and observed that many of the candles had gone out—on their own, or because Margaret had extinguished them to save them for another night. The fire burned low, but shed just enough light that Will could see all four corners of the main room and into the hallway that led back to his bedchamber and the spare room. Before he could say anything, Margaret shushed him, placing a finger to his lips. She then pointed to the door and beyond.

Will might have expected screaming or roaring—the sounds he'd heard at Alvah's place. Instead, there was thumping, snapping, and something like the noise of sails being torn. There was also a strange, guttural muttering that was so deep it could only have come from the monster. This faded in and out, went away and came back, as if the beast was arguing with himself, but Will understood not a syllable of it. At one point, there was a long, human sigh, as of sadness or disappointment. Later came a sound Will could only describe as wet. After long minutes of this hellish tumult, the monster began gibbering, almost laughing. The cottage's residents searched one another's eyes for comfort, assurance, any trace of confidence that the worst part of the night had passed. Nowhere could they find it, though. Especially not within themselves.

In time, Will held his breath and put an ear to the door. Xander, seeing his own opportunity, did the same, albeit much lower on the door's surface.

"Well?" Margaret whispered.

Will shook his head. He'd heard nothing. He passed his pistol to Margaret and said, "I'm opening the door." Xander stepped back and picked up his musket, allowing Will room to remove the timber barring the door. Again, Will held his breath, moving with the patience of sunset, so as not to make any noises that might alert the monster of his presence. When the door was fully unlocked, he eased it open just far enough to peek through the crack. The yard was bathed in moonlight. The palisade, beyond, seemed intact and uncompromised. Will reached back with his hand, wordlessly, and Margaret put the pistol into his waiting palm. He could feel his companions drawing close behind him, their breath on his neck. Slowly, by degrees, he nudged the door farther open with the toe of his boot. The hinges squeaked ever-so-slightly, and Will froze. He could feel his heartbeat pounding in his throat, taste blood in his mouth. *There is no greater hell than to be a prisoner of fear.*

He stepped through the door. Since the move hadn't cost him his life, he took another step, and then a third. Away from the cottage now, he could see the full moon blazing down upon his property. It knew what was transpiring on either side of the palisade, but remained aloof, kept its own counsel, and shared its secret knowledge with no one. Will scowled at it. There was a light wind, too, that was chilly enough for late October to raise gooseflesh. Every now and then, Will heard leaves skittering across the dead grass, but of the monster, nothing.

Margaret moved a pace or two off to Will's left, and Xander, to his right, so that they formed a phalanx in miniature. Behind the boy, Will saw, Sir Doggles battled pitifully with his own fears, wanting to protect his masters, but also desperate to run and hide. Collectively, they were not enough to kill the beast, Will felt with a dreadful certainty, unless they were lucky enough to put all three shots in its head. He tried to convince himself that was possible and found his performance wanting.

Ten paces or so from the palisade wall, they were assaulted with the smell of blood, of bile, of shit and piss. Will held up a hand to stop his companions, and they stood, listening, for several minutes before moving forward again.

At the wall, Will found a space to spy through, but could

make no immediate sense of what he saw. Xander was about to ask when Margaret, not ungently, put a hand over his mouth. Will moved down the wall and peered through another gap. Two minutes later, he repeated the process until he reached the gate. As before, he passed his pistol to Margaret and prepared to lift the bar from the gate.

He paused for a moment to steady himself, for he had never felt such abject terror. In the next instant, he might have his head torn off, or his bowels ripped open and flung up into his face. He might be ripped in half or lose an arm or a leg. Worse, the creature might break his back, leaving him paralyzed and forced to watch and listen as his family was slaughtered and devoured.

Almost, he laughed at himself. He'd never been accused him of lacking imagination. On this occasion, though, he would have sacrificed a good bit of it for some peace of mind.

He opened the gate.

The ground in front of him was a swamp of reddish-black and white. Steam rose from the remains of the dead—scant though they were—and it was nearly impossible to tell one lump of flesh from another. The carnage was spread out over a half circle, widening out from the wall some fifteen or twenty feet in all directions. Here, a fragment of bone caught the moonlight; there, a somewhat spherical shape that may have been part of a head. There were other, larger remnants, too, that might have been sections of torso or legs or...

To their credit, neither Margaret nor Xander cried out or vomited. And yet, Will could not rightly have called that a good thing.

With utmost care, he walked the perimeter of the area and found what he was looking for: Grendel's gory tracks, meandering off towards the forest with an almost careless whimsy that suggested he was, as hoped, utterly in the throes of his victims' opium-saturated blood.

A raven cried unexpectedly, and the noise was almost enough to make Will, Margaret, Xander and Sir Doggles abandon their quest and rush back into the cottage. Looking down, Will noticed his hands trembling terribly. His legs, he knew, were no better.

Nothing charged towards him from the distant trees. The raven squawked again, and the chill breeze rustled through the dead grass, but otherwise all was still.

Will resumed stalking the beast. The farther he got from the safety of the cottage, the more certain of his impending death he became, although it felt no less likely if he turned tail and ran back home. He advanced. After another fifteen or twenty paces, he heard the strange chuffing from earlier. Another five paces revealed something dark, lying in the moonlight some ways off. He glanced back at his companions, who followed his gaze and confirmed his vision. As one, they raised their weapons.

Within ten paces of the beast, they began to get a sense of its size, which was, as they'd suspected, immense. It gave off an odor, too, unlike that of any animal or man Will had ever smelled, pungent, yet earthy.

Margaret nudged Will in the ribs and mouthed, "Shoot it."

In response, he held up one finger. Wait.

The thing's feet were predictably enormous and almost manlike, though one had far too many toes. The skin beneath its fur—hair?—was dark and scaly. Will had never seen, never heard of any creature that had both hair and scales...unless the scales were the result of some strange disease. Farther up the legs, the hair became denser, especially around the reproductive organs marking it as male, decidedly male. The monster's distended belly, packed with the Newgate villains, was slick with blood and worse. Above that belly, a barrel-shaped chest, speckled with bits of half-eaten flesh, heaved like a bellows. Across its surface, too, was ample evidence of old injuries—scars, wounds, burns. Two massive arms stretched out to either side, caked in *coagulate gore*, and covered in odd spurs and barbs. The hands were more like claws or talons, each finger ending in a long, terrible scythe.

But it was the monster's visage that topped all previous horrors, for it was not that of an animal, wild and unknowable, or else some ancient fiend, but instead the face of an infant with more than a touch of the cretin. Shockingly, his eyes were of the palest blue, and he rolled them to-and-fro as if he'd lost all control of them. Upon spying Will and his friends, the beast broke into a wide, befuddled grin, his jagged teeth and horrible tusks still drenched in blood, and commenced a terrible mewling, broken up on occasion with an equally bizarre and incongruous chuckling.

"He's a child," Xander breathed.

"He's drugged," said Margaret.

"He's a corpse," Will answered, pointing his musket at Grendel's eye.

"Dimbra?" the monster muttered. "Dimbra korgu?"

And in those syllables, Will lost his nerve.

"Why do you hesitate?" Margaret demanded. "Shoot him."

"Dimbra?"

Will pointed his chin at Grendel. "Those are words. Words!" he rasped. "Have you ever met an animal possessed of language? The secrets he must know!"

"I have," said Margaret. "Those men he ate."

"But…"

"Do not. Language or no, he's a monster and will kill us as surely as he did our predecessors if we give him the chance."

Will knew it to be true. He leaned in so the beast could see him better. "O, who art thou that lookst so terrible?"

A blast jolted Will from his complacence. Margaret had fired her own musket.

Briefly, the monster thrashed, his arms and legs twitching and flexing. But his face, around the new hole in his cheek, was now utterly blank. Will wasted no time in firing Xander's musket into that face, whereupon Grendel lay still at last. Finally, Will fired his pistol into the center of the great beast's chest.

They stood then, Will, Margaret and Xander and his dog, for a good long while, staring at the body in the cold moonlight, wondering and worrying, in awe of the unknown.

"I'm sure our gunfire has awakened folks back in the village," Margaret ventured.

"Let them come, if they dare," said Will. "They left us alone to battle this creature. I'll apologize to no one."

Xander spoke up. "What do with we do with him?"

"I'll take his head into town in the morning, if one of you will fetch me the axe."

"And the rest of him?"

"Leave him where he lies. The governor and his men will want to investigate."

"Can it not wait until the sun is up?" Margaret countered.

"I'll do it now," was all Will said in reply.

~ 34 ~

AND I'LL BE WISE HEREAFTER
AND SEEK FOR GRACE

Jamestown, October/November, 1619

A gain, sleep did not visit the cottage, but Will and Xander were on the road early, carrying the huge head between them in a sack.

"Do you think there be more of these?" Xander asked as they walked along.

"I cannot think otherwise."

"What will we do?"

"The three of us have played our parts. Now, the rest of the settlers have no choice but fight."

They dropped the head onto a large crate outside the church and removed its bloody covering. Passersby gasped or cried out in alarm, and a crowd began to gather.

"Is this the beast?" the governor's voice rang out in the crisp, autumn air.

Will turned to see the fellow striding casually in his direction. "One of them, at least." The comment had its desired effect, eliciting exclamations of fear and anger from the villagers. One woman, weeping uncontrollably, stepped forward to strike the head over and over until she had to be pulled away by friends.

For his part, Sir George shot Will a look of censure, mild but palpable. Will returned his glare unapologetically.

"Where is the rest of it?" the governor asked after several minutes.

"On my land, of course. It seems he came across some

brigands attempting to breach my palisade and...well, you can imagine the results."

"You're saying there are dead men on your property?"

"Pieces of 'em, anyway," Will replied.

The governor grimaced at this. "Allow me and my men to escort you and this...thing," he gestured to the head, "back to your land. I would see these dead you mention."

Sir George paced the scene of the massacre, poking and prodding at the remains of the dead ruffians as if he might revive them long enough to answer a question or two. His face fixed in a look of grim disgust, he turned to Will and said, "Quite a coincidence, isn't it? These men you claim have been hectoring you are eaten by our monster?"

Will was having none of it. "The Lord works in mysterious ways, does He not?"

"Hmmm," the governor replied. "How many men died here, do you reckon?"

"Three or four? You could always cut the beast open and count..."

Having examined the monster first, Sir George was in no hurry to return to its side. Instead, he packed his pipe and struck a flame to its contents. "You are not to be trifled with, Master Kemp. I see that now more than ever."

Will nodded. "I hope your House of Burgesses will lend more credence to my concerns henceforth."

"I doubt it not," the governor answered, puffing on his pipe, but never taking his eyes off Will. "At any rate, I am glad you finally caught and killed the bear."

"That's no bear," Xander protested.

"If I say it was a bear, look you," said Sir George, "it was a bear. The Virginia Company will brook no answer else."

"Bad for business?" Margaret asked.

"Just so." After a moment's thought, the governor added, "My men here will help you build a bonfire. There must be nothing left of the beast by evening."

It was too heavy, too unwieldly to lift onto the pyre, and so the group rolled Grendel's corpse into position, revealing, along the way, a large hump on the upper right side of its back, just as the natives' illustration had indicated. There was also a misshapen, vestigial third arm on the left side of its back, which made Will wonder about the creature's internal organs, whether it possessed more than one heart or something else, altogether alien. He was curious enough that he almost asked the men helping him to pause, that he might perform an informal autopsy and sketch out the monster's insides. But discretion, he recalled, was the better part of valor, and so he remained quiet.

It occurred to Will that he'd been in the New World for half a year. He could hardly recall or even imagine a more eventful time in his life, and that was saying something. He and his new family had faced grave challenges, and bested them all. They'd seen wonders, too, and surely there were more to come. But William had found his second chance, and if he was to end here, he was content it should be so. Still...

He had committed murder—whatever the justifications— and exposed a darkness within himself that left him fearful. The horrible truth was, he'd enjoyed exacting revenge upon the local ruffians and on Grendel, too. He'd enjoyed killing them. Had there been other options that he'd simply failed to see, or else ignored on purpose? What had he become? What was he becoming? He ruminated on his dark thane, on his halting, bunch-backed Richard, on Iago, and wondered if he was already past redemption.

Nor was he alone in darkness.

Sir George had overseen a sort of cover-up, a conspiracy of silence or misinformation that had preserved the colony's viability at the expense of lives. He was, therefore, no less a murderer than Will himself. There remained, too, the fates of Jamestown's new "servants" to consider. How long could Will tolerate a community that kept others as chattel? Finally, there was the question of Grendel's seemingly recent arrival in the area. How and why had he come, and had the Powhatans had anything to do with it?

Against that possibility, Will determined to make himself understood.

"I need your assistance," Will told his companions over the morning meal.

"In doing…?" Margaret asked.

"Taking Grendel's head to the Powhatans."

"But I thought you burned it with the body…"

"That was a bag of rubbish to deceive Sir George."

"But why take it to the natives now?"

"As a gift, a warning, who can say what they'll make of it?"

Xander stood up, as if ready to leave on the instant. "I'll go with you."

"And I," said Margaret, "Of course."

It was not as long a walk as Will had expected and certainly shorter than he'd hoped. But the natives were like good fortune, only to be found by happenstance but never when sought. Amongst the group that appeared in front of him was the werowance, himself. Will nodded to Xander, and both lowered their burden to the ground. After undoing the sack, Will stepped back from the head and allowed the Powhatans full view of it. Their reaction was immediate. Most of the natives jumped away. Only the werowance stood fast, his teeth bared and his fists clenched.

"He hunts us no more," Will offered by way of explanation.

Cautiously, the werowance and his fellows stepped forward to examine the head, poking it first with their spears and then one or two even beating it with their clubs. Will gestured to the head and then back to the werowance. "For you," he said.

The other man seemed to think for a moment before saying, "Yes. Good."

Perhaps Will was imagining it, but he thought he saw something in the natives' eyes—respect? Fear? He'd made his point, then. He meant them no harm, but if they came again unbidden onto his land, if they stole from him or tried again to lead Xander away, there would be consequences.

After some discussion amongst themselves, the werowance's warriors shoved two spears through Grendel's eyes and, with one man on the points and another on the spear butts, made to carry the head away.

"Wish I'd thought of that," Will muttered to Margaret. "Probably a lot easier on the back."

She laughed. "You were gifted with boundless imagination, my friend. But common sense...?"

Even Xander couldn't suppress a smile at this.

Before the Powhatans could disappear completely, Will called out to them. "Dimbra!" he said. "Dimbra korgu."

They paused and turned to look back at him, their expressions unreadable. The werowance spoke a single syllable, and his fellows resumed their journey. They did not vanish or fade into the wilderness but remained in plain sight until they were simply too far away to be seen at all.

By Hallowmas, tensions in the colony died down, as if the massacre had never happened, save that a few ne-er-do-wells had disappeared and, apparently, were little missed. Sometime later, the House of Burgesses formed a semi-permanent patrol against the arrival of other monsters and even went so far as to set traps and poison, but nothing came of their precautions, to everyone's relief.

Will stood just outside his cottage one morning, considering the frost on the yard's lone tree. In his hand, he held a mug of coffee, which sent tendrils of steam dancing up into the morning air. Captain Smith had introduced the stuff to the colony, and it was damned near impossible to start one's day without it. Margaret placed herself just behind Will, her arms wrapped around his belly in a comfortable, contented embrace.

"No words for an autumn morning?" she asked.

"Mmmm," he intoned.

"Then belike your son hath a few. Xander!" She turned her head towards the cottage door, and the young man, on cue, emerged with a slender book in hand. With a signal from Margaret, he opened it and began to read aloud.

"That time of year thou mayst in me be...behold
When yellow leaves, or none, or few, do hang
Upon those boogs which shake against the cold,
Bare ruin'd ch...choirs, where late the sweet birds sang.

In me thou see'st the twi..twilight of such day
As after sunset fadeth in the west,
Which by and by black night doth take away,
Death's second self, that seals up all in rest.
In me thou see'st the glowing of such fire
That on the ashes of his you…th doth lie,
As the death-bed where…on it must expire,
Consum'd with that which it was nourish'd by.
This thou perceiv'st, which makes thy love more strong,
To love that well which thou must leave ere long."

Such joy rushed up William's chest, from heart into throat, that he could not for several seconds reply for fear of embarrassing himself and his son with wracking sobs. The lad could read! He'd learned to read. Will could not speak, no, but he embraced young Xander as if the boy had somehow saved his father's life. Margaret then joined in the embrace, and the three stood thus, happily, for long, long minutes. Only Sir Doggles' bark broke them apart.

"We'd never forget you, silly dog!" said Xander, as he stooped down to pat the beast with his free hand.

Watching them, Will had an epiphany.

"He is thine," Luce had said, and he'd taken that to mean the boy was literally his son. Now, he understood that she'd offered him as a gift, the way one offers up one's soul to a lover. In Xander, she'd entrusted Will with the most important thing in her life, her greatest achievement and, doubtless, her greatest love. Immediately, he was overcome. On the one hand, he was ashamed at having mistaken Luce's message; on the other, he was humbled by the depth of her trust and the magnitude of her gift.

AFTERWORD

You will notice an endless number of quotes from Shakespeare's (and sometimes his peers') work in this book. I have intentionally decided not to cite them for two reasons: one, I did not want to distract the reader from the flow of the narrative, and two, I felt if it makes you look these up yourself, you'll have gained more than a simple citation.

As to the historical authenticity of the baseline elements of this story, a man and woman named William and Margaret Kemp *did* sail from England to Jamestown in 1619 aboard the George. Shakespeare *did* have a colleague named Will Kemp of whom, if scholars are to be believed, he was not overly fond. There *was* an African prostitute named Lucy or Luce, whom some historians and academics believe to have been the famed Dark Lady of the Sonnets. Opium was not widely known or used as medicine for pain relief in England until 1680...but that does not mean it was unknown in the streets by or before 1619. Flintlocks *were* in existence by 1619, but terribly rare, though not, perhaps, beyond the reach of a wealthy celebrity.

ACKNOWLEDGMENTS

This novel would never have been completed without the wit, wisdom, and unflagging enthusiasm of Austin Tichenor, of the Reduced Shakespeare Company and TheShakespeareance. com

Others who played roles include, in no particular order:

Gillian Batchelder
Christopher Selbie
Gary Logan
Chris Harris
Barry Kraft
Mark Cuddy
Michael Fleming

And, of course, I must thank my cover artist, Felix Ortiz, and my publishers at Crossroad Press.

ABOUT THE AUTHOR

A llan is a professional actor, educator, writer and former stand-up comedian. During his years on stage, he's gotten to participate in countless battles—some even with other people—involving longswords, rapiers, daggers, staves, pistols, bottles, loaves of French bread and, of course, his grimy little fists. Allan is a lifelong fan of epic fantasy and horror, so you can just imagine how much he loves Grimdark. Allan lives in Seattle, within a few miles of the two richest men on Earth and can thereby assure you that there's no such thing as financial osmosis.

BOOKS BY ALLAN BATCHELDER

The Immortal Treachery Series:
Steel, Blood & Fire
As Flies to Wanton Boys
Corpse Cold
The Abject God
The End of All Things
This Thing of Darkness

To learn more, follow us on Twitter at @TarmunVykers
On Facebook at www.facebook.com/SteelBloodFire
Or at www.immortaltreachery.com

Curious about other Crossroad Press books?
Stop by our site:
http://store.crossroadpress.com
We offer quality writing
in digital, audio, and print formats.

Made in the USA
Monee, IL
29 August 2022

12760029R10132